28.95 DATE DUE

The
DARK
ISLAND

**Center Point
Large Print**

**This Large Print Book carries the
Seal of Approval of N.A.V.H.**

ॐ श्री गणेशाय नमः

ROBERT J. CONLEY

The
DARK
ISLAND

CENTER POINT PUBLISHING
THORNDIKE, MAINE

This Center Point Large Print edition
is published in the year 2003 by arrangement with
The Oklahoma University Press.

The text of this Large Print edition is unabridged. In other
aspects, this book may vary from the original edition. Printed in
Thailand. Set in 16-point Times New Roman type by
Bill Coskrey and Gary Socquet.

ISBN 1-58547-256-5

Library of Congress Cataloging-in-Publication Data.

Conley, Robert J.
    The dark island / Robert J. Conley.--Center Point large print ed.
    p. cm.
    ISBN 1-58547-256-5 (lib. bdg. : alk. paper)
    1. Cherokee Indians--Fiction. 2. Large type books. I. Title.

PS3553.O494 D36 2003
813'.54--dc21

2002073558

The
DARK
ISLAND

ONE

ASQUANI, the young man who had been raised as one of *Ani-yunwi-ya,* the Real People, sat alone on top of the high hill just outside the town of Kituwah. He was sad, and he was feeling sorry for himself. He had felt sorry for himself most of his life, ever since he had been old enough to realize that he was not really one of the Real People.

His father, the man he called father, known as the Carrier, was one of the Real People, but he was only the adopted father of 'Squani. Carrier had rescued 'Squani's mother, Potmaker, a Timucua woman, from the Spaniards in a place far to the south, a place the Spaniards called Florida, and she had been pregnant at the time by one of her captors. So 'Squani's mother was a Timucua woman, and his father, whose identity was unknown, was a Spaniard.

And 'Squani did not look like one of the Real People. His skin was lighter than most of theirs, and his hair was of a different hue and texture, reddish and a little wavy. His eyes, too, were light, almost gray. And even though he had a perfectly good given name, the Real People all called him Asquani, or 'Squani, their way of pronouncing the word *Español,* a Spaniard.

Very often, 'Squani knew, when the Real People brought in among them an outsider, one of the seven clans would adopt that person in order to make him into one of them. 'Squani had heard stories about a man who had been called the Shawnee. The *Ani-Sawahani* man, an enemy of the Real People, had originally been brought among them as a captive, but eventually even he had been adopted by a clan.

Potmaker, however, had never been adopted. 'Squani wondered sometimes if that was because she had never quite mastered the language of the Real People. She had learned to speak it, of course, but with a strange-sounding Timucuan accent.

At other times 'Squani would think that he himself must be the reason. None of the seven clans, he thought, would want to count a Spaniard among their number, and since, among the Real People, a child belongs to its mother's clan, 'Squani would have automatically belonged to any clan that adopted Potmaker. Probably, he thought, especially in his most self-pitying moments, that was the real reason no clan had chosen to adopt his mother.

He knew, of course, why the Real People hated the Spaniards so much. He had heard often enough the tale of the trip his adopted father had made to Florida, and how he had found the Spaniards there attacking villages of Timucua people with no provocation, killing some, taking others as slaves. 'Squani's own mother had been one of those captives, and the very existence of 'Squani himself was a direct result of their repeated abuse of her. Because of that, he often thought that even she, his own mother, must secretly hate him.

And he had also heard about the long travels of the Spaniard De Soto, the towns and villages he had burned along the way, the tremendous numbers of people he had killed and the cruel ways in which he had killed them. The Real People had been lucky. De Soto had barely touched their country, but he had devastated much of the country to their south and southwest. And all because of a crazy lust for the yellow metal. 'Squani wondered sometimes what it was about the yellow metal that was so important to his father's people.

And then the old man, Deadwood Lighter, one of the Real People, a priest, a *Kutani,* who had seemingly vanished some years earlier, had returned to the Real People after his long absence. He had gone west with two other priests to search for the home of Thunder and bring back the rain, but they had been captured by some strange and fierce people in the west. One of them had been killed, and one had escaped and returned home just at the time the people had risen up against the priests and killed them all. All except those three.

After a while, everyone had assumed that Deadwood Lighter was dead. But then he had returned. He had been sold as a slave to the Spaniards, and he had been with De Soto on the entire trip. He had told the whole horrible story to all of the people in vivid detail. And he had warned the Real People to be prepared for the return of the Spaniards and to be prepared to defend themselves against their brutality. So 'Squani knew well why the Real People hated the Spaniards, hated and feared them so.

'Squani was also a Spaniard, and so they hated him. At least, he imagined that they did. Wherever he went, he felt their stares. He had no friends, and he had no woman. At his age he should have had a woman, and he felt as if the people were talking about him behind his back because he did not have one. He knew that the reason he did not have a woman was because he was a Spaniard, but sometimes he worried that the people would think there were other reasons, that perhaps he did not care for women, when, of course, he did. But what woman of the Real People would want a Spaniard for her man?

And the more he thought about his miserable condition and brooded over it, the more Spanish he felt. But of course, he had no idea what it really meant to feel Spanish, to be Spanish. He had been raised as one of the Real People, and he had never even seen a Spaniard. That was the reason he had gone to the old man.

"Teach me to speak their language," he had begged. He had been afraid to tell Deadwood Lighter the real reason he wanted to learn, how he really felt about his own identity, so he had added, "If they come back, like you said, someone will need to know how to speak to them."

'Squani was already something of an accomplished linguist. His mother had taught him her own Timucua tongue, and he had learned to speak the trade language with which the different peoples who lived in that area, the Real People, the Choctaw People, the Chickasaw People and others, communicated with each other across linguistic barriers. He could also read and write, but that was a secret.

For the Carrier, his adopted father, had taken him out some years before, when 'Squani had been but a boy, pretending to go on a hunt. When they were safely alone, Carrier had sworn him to secrecy, and he had been so serious about it that it had frightened the boy just a little.

"In the days of the *Ani-Kutani*," Carrier had then said, "in the days when the priests had absolute rule over the lives of the Real People, there were some priests among them who could write our language."

'Squani did not know what that meant, "to write," and so Carrier had explained to him how different marks stood for different sounds, and how a person could memorize the marks and then be able to write down anything that he could say. And if another person also memorized the marks in the same way, then that person would be able to read back the same words the other had written down.

"When the people rose up against the priests and killed them," he continued, "the writing would have been lost forever. But there were three priests who had gone west on a mission. One of them was my uncle, Dancing Rabbit, whom you know. When he returned and learned what had happened here during his long absence, he was afraid that someone would kill him, too, but they'd had enough of killing by then, I guess.

"Anyway, Dancing Rabbit was one who knew the writing. He was afraid to say anything about it openly, though, for fear that it would arouse the old hatreds and suspicions, but he took me into the woods, just as I have now taken you.

"He told me that the writing is very important to us. It's sacred, and it must be saved. But it's also very dangerous just now. We have to save it in secret. Someday, when the Real People have forgotten about the *Ani-Kutani,* when the old hatreds are dead, the one who knows the writing will be able to give it out again to all the Real People.

"In the meantime, we must preserve it. When you have mastered it, and when you get older, you will do as I have done and select a boy to teach it to, perhaps your own son, perhaps a nephew. You'll know whom to choose when the

13

time comes."

Carrier had then begun to teach the writing to 'Squani, and 'Squani had learned all of the symbols quickly and easily. So he could speak three languages, and he could read and write one of them, and now he wanted to add one more to his list: *Español,* the language of the Spaniards, the language of his mysterious and unknown father.

And Deadwood Lighter had at last agreed to teach him, and every day after that, he and 'Squani would meet, and they would talk in Spanish, and Deadwood Lighter had said that 'Squani was a very good pupil. He praised the young man for his pronunciation, saying that he sounded almost like a real Spaniard. And then one day, suddenly and unexpectedly, the old man had died.

'Squani was devastatcd by the old man's passing. He was sad, and he felt very much alone. He had grown close to the old man, even fond of him. But perhaps even more devastating to the young man was the sad fact that he would no longer have anyone with whom he could converse in Spanish, the language of his father, the language he had lately begun to feel was his own. And he had not yet learned enough from the old man about the Spaniards themselves.

During their Spanish language lessons, Deadwood Lighter had told 'Squani things about the people whose language they were using. He had told him about their strange beliefs and their habits. He had told him about their religion, and how it was all explained in a big book filled with writing in the Spanish language.

"You mean," 'Squani had said, "that the Spaniards can write their language down?" He had almost said, "the way we do," but he had stopped himself in time. "I'd like to learn to read and write it, too," he had said instead. But that had not come about. Deadwood Lighter had died quietly in the night. They made a funeral for him there in Kituwah, and the people all mourned for him the way they should. But 'Squani mourned longer and more deeply than all the others, for he mourned a greater personal loss than did they. He had not lost just a friend. He had lost his only friend. He had lost the one person who had given meaning to his lonely life.

So 'Squani sat alone there on the hill. He was sad over the death of Deadwood Lighter, and he was feeling sorry for himself, 'Squani, the misplaced Spaniard, the man with no home and no purpose.

TWO

I T was after dark when 'Squani finally climbed down the hill and went back inside the walls of Kituwah. He had not walked very far into the town before he realized that something out of the ordinary was going on. Curious, he walked on, but he changed his direction. Instead of heading for home, he walked toward the townhouse. Sure enough, he found a meeting in progress there. He stepped into the doorway, and he felt immediately as if all eyes turned toward him. He moved to a spot just inside the doorway and to his left, and he squatted down there, leaning back against the wall. The meeting continued, but 'Squani still felt as if people were staring at him, or at least, sneaking sly and furtive looks. He tried to ignore them and listen to discover what the meeting was all about.

"The old man warned us that this would happen," he heard someone say. "Now that it has actually come about, what do we do?"

"But they're not close to us," said another. "They're clear on the other side of the country of the Catawbas, on an island out in the big water. We don't have to do anything about it. Not yet."

Then 'Squani saw Trotting Wolf move up to the place for speaking. Trotting Wolf was a prominent leader of the Wolf Clan, and 'Squani was secretly envious of the man's position and reputation. He would have liked the same kind of prominence for himself; but, of course, a man without a clan had no way to advance his status among the Real People.

Everyone was quiet there in the townhouse, waiting to hear what Trotting Wolf would have to say. The man stood up as tall as he could, taking a deep breath to swell his chest. Holding his head high, he slowly looked over the crowd. He wore beautifully decorated leggings and moccasins, and a matchcoat of tightly woven turkey feathers was draped over one shoulder. All of Trotting Wolf's skin that was exposed to view was covered in tattoos which told of his exploits in war, and several scars were also visible, further evidence of his battle experience. His head was shaved except for the scalp lock which grew long out of the top of his head and hung loose all the way down his back.

Up toward the top of the scalp lock, a lone eagle feather was tied in his hair. It dangled upside down along the left side of Trotting Wolf's head. Around his neck was a thong from which a shell gorget depended, covering his sternum.

On the gorget was incised the figure of a dancing man. In one hand the figure brandished a huge ball-headed war club. In the other he held by its scalp lock a severed head. At last Trotting Wolf spoke.

"I speak here for *Ani-Wahya*," he said, "my people, the Wolf People. When the old man told us that they would be coming back, the *Ani-Asquani,* the Wolf People came forward. We said that we would guard the passes that lead into this mountain country of ours. We would keep out all strangers. Now that these white men have come back, we will do that. It may be true, as we've heard, that they are not yet near our country, but we've also heard that they move fast on their beasts. They could come riding through the Catawba country at any time. We, the Wolf People, will be watching for them. We will be ready."

There was more talk, but 'Squani was no longer listening. His heart was beating fast with excitement. So the Spaniards were back. They were only across the Catawba country and a little ways off the edge of the world on a small island there in the water. It was the best news he had ever heard. He longed to see them.

And he had another thought. With the Spaniards so close and possibly posing a new threat to the Real People, the suspicions and resentment, hatred even, that was normally directed at 'Squani would almost certainly intensify. Life in Kituwah, in any of the towns of the Real People, would become, if such a thing were possible, even more intolerable for him than it had been before. Then, once again, the voice of Trotting Wolf intruded on his thoughts.

"When the sun comes out again from under the eastern edge of the great sky vault," he said, "the Wolf People will go out from here to all the towns of the Real People. They will tell the Wolf People in those other towns. All of the passes into our country will be closed to outsiders before the end of the day. All will be closely guarded by the Wolf People."

Then 'Squani came to a sudden and bold decision, so sudden that he was not even conscious of having given it any thought. He would go to the Spaniards. He was not welcome in Kituwah. He was not liked. He had never been wanted, and so he would not be missed. He might even be safer getting out of the reach of the Real People, now that they were so wrought up over the nearness of the Spaniards. His Spanish blood might be enough to bring about his untimely death at the hands of some overzealous patriot. Perhaps the Spaniards, on the other hand, would welcome him, since his real father was one of them. Deadwood Lighter had told him that among the Spaniards one's father was more important than one's mother. Perhaps his father would even be there among them on the island.

The talking went on in the townhouse, but 'Squani had heard all that he was interested in hearing. He stood up and slipped out the door. He hoped that no one noticed, but he thought that probably they had. They were always staring at him. He hurried through the streets until he came to his mother's house, and he ducked his head to go through the small doorway.

It was dark inside the small house, but he knew where to find everything he needed. He would have to hurry. He did not want to see anyone and have to explain his actions, and he did not want to encounter the members of the Wolf Clan in the pass on his way out of the territory of the Real People.

He found his leggings and started to put them on, but he changed his mind. He didn't want to waste any time. He spread a soft tanned deerskin on the floor, and he laid out the leggings on that. He put his extra pair of moccasins on there, too. He put a folded matchcoat on the skin and a pair of mittens. He found a pouch of tobacco, which also contained a short, clay pipe, and another pouch of dried corn, and he put those down. Then he rolled up the deerskin and tied it with leather thongs.

He found his bow and arrows, a blowgun and some darts, his flint knife and his war club. The knife and club were secured with a sash around his waist, and the deerskin bundle slung over his shoulder. The arrows in a quiver were also slung over his shoulder. The darts were tucked into a rawhide band which was wrapped tightly around the blowgun itself. He picked up the blowgun and the bow and ducked through the doorway.

The meeting must still be going on, he thought, for still he saw no one in the streets. Good, he thought. Keeping to the darkest shadows, he headed for the opening in the wall, the way out of the town.

He felt a sudden desperation, like a need to escape from a place in which he had been confined against his will, and he moved as quickly as he could. He reached the place where the two ends of the wall began to overlap each other in order to create the long passageway into or out of the town, and he ran through, feeling with every step that someone might suddenly appear in his path to block his way, to stop him, to strike him down and perhaps even to kill him.

But of course, no one did. And soon he found himself outside the wall. Still he ran. He wanted to get as far away from Kituwah as possible before anyone missed him and came after him, and he wanted to get clear out of the country of the Real People before the self-appointed Wolf guardians of the passes began to take up their stations, for they, too, might try to stop him. He had heard Trotting Wolf say that they would close the passes. They would let no one in. Did it also mean that they would let no one out? Especially a hated Spaniard?

He ran along a road that went generally east and would lead him eventually into the Catawba country. He would have to slow his pace once he crossed into that land, for the Catawbas and the Real People, though not at present engaged in open warfare, were not on friendly terms. But he wouldn't be there for a while, so that was not yet a real worry. He ran.

The road began to descend. He was going down the mountain toward the plain. He ran faster, until he stumbled and fell, rolling over and over uncontrollably. He rolled off the edge of the road and nearly fell down the steep edge of the hillside along which the road ran. Just in the nick of time, he grabbed at a clump of brush and caught himself. His bow went flying down the hillside in the darkness.

He pulled himself up and stood on unsteady legs in the middle of the road once again. Then he realized that he had also lost his blowgun and darts. He checked the quiver on his back. It was empty. He took it off and tossed it to the side of the road. At least the bundle was still on his back.

He felt at his waist and found the flint knife. It was safe, but the war club was gone. Silently, he chided himself for having been so foolish. In his haste he had lost almost all of his weapons. He wondered for a moment if he should give up his plan and return to Kituwah, but he dismissed that cowardly thought from his mind.

He had made a decision, and he would stick to it. He would find other weapons, or make them, or he would manage without them. He was not going to fight with the Spaniards, after all. He was going to join them. But the Catawbas, that would be a different story. Well, he would just have to be very careful, avoiding the Catawbas and sneaking through their country undetected if he could.

Forced to stop his headlong run, he paused for a moment to reflect, and one result of that moment of reflection was that he began to feel the bruises and bumps and scratches he had received in his fall.

"I have enough of a head start now, anyway," he told himself. "It's still dark. I'll travel more slowly."

He began walking along the road, still going down the mountain, and the bruises and scratches made the walking painful. He noticed that he was limping just a little. He began to feel dejected. His trip had only just begun, and he had already lost almost all of his weapons, and he had managed to hurt himself. This trip was not going the way he had imagined that it would.

By the time the sun was beginning to brighten the sky along the eastern horizon, 'Squani was tired and hungry. He made his way down the side of the hill to the creek that ran along there. He knelt down and took a drink. The water was clear and cold, but it did nothing for his hunger.

He stood up again and took the bundle off his back. Then he stripped off his breechclout and moccasins and waded in to bathe himself, At first, the cold water was a shock, but soon it began to soothe his aching body. He washed off the dust and dirt and bathed his wounds.

He drank some more water, but it only served to emphasize his hunger, so he got out of the water and unrolled the deerskin bundle to take out his pouch of dried corn.

It wasn't the tastiest meal he had ever eaten, nor the most filling, but it did take the sharp edge off his hunger, and by the time he had finished eating, the sun had dried him well enough so that he could dress. He put on his leggings as well as his breechclout and moccasins, and then he rolled up his remaining belongings again in the deerskin and slung the bundle once again across his back.

He looked around, wishing for a bow and some arrows, then shrugged and climbed back up to the road. He still had a long and dangerous walk ahead of him. It had only just begun.

THREE

IT was midday. 'Squani looked up and saw the sun almost directly overhead. The Real People said that she stopped there in the middle of each day to visit at her daughter's house. But Deadwood Lighter had told him that the Spaniards did not believe that the sun was a female, or that she was alive. She was a ball of fire, and she circled around the world from her place far out in the sky, which was not, as the Real People believed, a great rock vault. It was rather nothing but vast space. He wondered who was right about all that, and he decided that he was inclined to believe the Spaniards. He longed to be with them and to learn more.

Then his thoughts were interrupted by the sounds of people coming toward him. They were on the road ahead of him. He could tell. He ran to his right, off the road and into the cover of some thick brush. He hid himself there, as well as he could, and waited.

The people came closer, and 'Squani could see them through the brush. There were men, women and children. Some of the adults seemed quite old. What kind of a group was this, he wondered. They came closer, slowly, for they moved like people who had been long on the road. Moved slowly, wearily, almost painfully, as if each step hurt more than the last. Their faces were long and drawn with suffering. Still, 'Squani did not move.

As the wretched-looking bunch passed by him, he heard a child whine something to one of the adults, and he did not understand the language. 'Squani decided that they must be refugees, but from where? And where did they think they were going? As far as 'Squani could tell, they were headed for the country of the Real People, and just now, he thought, the Real People were not in the mood to receive strangers kindly.

Well, it was not his worry, he told himself. For all he knew, the pathetic group might be some bitter enemy of the Real People, and whether they were friends or enemies mattered little to 'Squani. He had already made up his mind. He had turned his back on the Real People and was going to cast his lot with the people of his father, the people whose name he carried, *Ani-'squani.* He kept still and watched the refugees disappear down the road.

When at last they were gone, he moved back out onto the

road. As he continued on toward the east, he tried not to think about the pitiful refugees, but he could not get the image of the pathetic, slow-moving group out of his mind. Still, he moved ahead. He resolved to be strong in this. He would not allow feelings of pity to slow him down or turn him back. He was dealing with his own problems. Let them deal with theirs.

Trotting Wolf moved up the side of the mountain. Close behind him came two more Wolf People. One was called the Howler and the other He-Kills-Quickly. All three men were heavily armed. It was a long and steep climb, yet the three men took it easily, even though they were not young. At last they reached the top. Trotting Wolf stood up straight and looked around. The other two looked at him and then at each other.

"Where are they?" asked He-Kills-Quickly.

"They're here," said Trotting Wolf. "We'll wait for them here."

"Maybe something happened to them," said the Howler, "or maybe they decided to move to another location where they can see better."

"Be patient," said Trotting Wolf. "They're here, and right now, they're watching us, I think."

Just then there was a movement ahead of them and to their right, a faint rustling of brush. The two men behind Trotting Wolf reached for their war clubs. Trotting Wolf simply stood still. Where the brush rustled, a man appeared.

" *'Siyo,* " he called out. "Is it Trotting Wolf?"

"Yes," said Trotting Wolf, "and the Howler and He-

Kills-Quickly. Come out and join us."

The man came out from behind the rock, and almost immediately three others appeared and followed him. They walked over to join Trotting Wolf and his two companions.

"Have you seen anyone from up here?" Trotting Wolf asked.

"No one has tried to come in," said the other. "We only saw Asquani traveling east. He was alone."

"Hm," Trotting Wolf mused. "I knew that he had left his home. I wonder where he's going. His parents are worried, I know. Well, you four have been here long enough. We three will take your place now. Go on home and eat and rest."

"It has been a long time. It would be good if we had some others to help us watch the passes."

"Yes," said Trotting Wolf, "it would be good, but we have to do the job with what we have. We *Ani-Wahya* took on the responsibility, and we will not ask for help from the other clans."

"No. Of course not," said the other, and he and his three comrades took their leave and headed down the mountainside. They had not gone far when Trotting Wolf's voice stopped them.

"High Back," called Trotting Wolf.

The man in the rear stopped and looked back over his shoulder.

"What is it?" he asked.

"Be sure to tell the parents of the young man 'Squani that you saw him going off this way."

"Yes," said High Back. "We will."

Trotting Wolf watched the others leave. Then he walked around until he found a vantage point which afforded him a wide view of the pass below. He saw no signs of human life down there, but he knew that there were still Spaniards in the area, and the Real People had decided to allow no strangers into their lands. He and the other Wolf People would have to watch constantly. His tired clan brother, High Back, had been right. It would be good to have more help with this task.

'Squani did not know exactly where he was. He knew that he was well out of the territory of the Real People, and he knew that he was still headed east. He did not know whose land he was in. Nor did he know how much farther it was to the coast and the island which he sought. There was nothing he could do but to keep moving east. Sooner or later, he would come to the edge of the land, to the big water. He would have to.

The road he walked rose slightly ahead of him, and as he reached the top of the rise, he saw down below him, in the valley ahead there next to the river, a palisaded town. His first reaction was panic, and he ran to the side of the road. The hillside rose sharply there and was covered with thick woods.

'Squani made his way into the cover of the forested mountainside and held still for a moment until he felt quite safe. Then he began to ease himself forward, keeping in the dark cover of the trees. The going was slow, for the ground was rough, and the way was constantly winding around obstacles, trees and brush, rocks and fallen branches.

But soon 'Squani found himself in a better spot from which to spy on the village. He positioned himself as best he could, and then he watched. He saw no one moving around outside the walls. That, he thought, was a little unusual for the middle of the day.

But there was something else, and he couldn't quite decide what it was. Something about the picture did not seem quite right. He moved farther up the hillside, but the height did not improve his view of the scene below. After moving around a little more, he decided to climb a tree.

He located one with a thick trunk and low branches, and soon he was up the tree a distance of about three times his own height. From there, he could see over the wall of the town below. Still he saw no one. No one at all. There were no men hanging around the townhouse and no women outside their own houses, no children playing in the streets. There were no dogs, even. The town was deserted.

'Squani got down out of the tree and worked his way through the woods and back to the road. Then he walked down toward the empty town. Still he moved cautiously and easily, and as he drew closer to the town, he grew more nervous. But no one appeared. Nothing happened. He arrived at the wall, and he made his way to the opening that would allow him to enter. He hesitated there for a moment, looking around, then took a deep breath and sidled in, keeping his back to the wall.

Soon he relaxed, for once inside the walls of the town, it became obvious to 'Squani that the place had been deserted for some time. It appeared to him that he was probably the first human being to move inside those walls for many days, months perhaps. He wondered what had happened there to make the people leave their homes.

The town was similar to the towns of the Real People, but the houses were round rather than rectangular and bark-covered rather than plastered with mud. 'Squani knew, of course, that abandoned towns were not unusual. People often moved their towns when the ground of their garden plots needed a rest. And he knew from the stories that Deadwood Lighter had told that the Spaniards led by the man called De Soto had caused many towns to be abandoned.

Yet this deserted and neglected place gave him a strange and uneasy feeling, and he could not say why. He walked slowly to the nearest house and cautiously peered inside. It was dark in there, and it took a moment for his eyes to adjust to the change. The house was empty. He moved on down the lane to the next house.

When he stuck his head through the door of the second house, there was a quick scampering sound, and it made him jump back away from the doorway. Then he realized that it had probably been some small animal which had made its home in there. He looked again. There was a broken pot in one corner. Nothing more. Whatever little creature he had frightened had gotten itself safely away.

Somewhere behind him a crow called out loudly, and it sounded to 'Squani as if he were being harshly criticized for his intrusion into the silent solitude of this mysterious town. He moved on.

He walked past several houses, and then found himself standing in front of the large townhouse. He looked around for a moment, then went inside. At first he thought that it, too, was empty, and he was about to decide that the town had simply been abandoned when its inhabitants had decided to move to a new location, probably because of the land. They had packed up everything and moved. Otherwise, he thought, there would be more things lying around. Then he noticed something in a far corner.

He walked slowly across the room toward the object. About halfway over, he could see that it was the decayed remains of a human being. He felt a shudder of horror and revulsion, but he braced himself and walked closer. The clothing was strange, not like anything he had seen before.

A Spaniard?

His heart thrilled, and he moved closer. Then he could see that the neglected body was horribly decayed and lying in a painfully distorted position. He leaned forward to look more closely, and then he noticed that the skull was broken, crushed, as if it had been bashed in by a heavy war club.

So there *had* been a fight here. Probably the Spaniards had chased the inhabitants out of the town. This one had been killed and left behind. The survivors from the town had most likely returned later to take proper care of their own dead. He wondered why the Spaniards had not done likewise for this one.

He squatted down, leaning his elbows on his knees, and for a long moment he stared, fascinated, at the ghastly remains there before him. He eyed the clothing mostly, especially the hard-looking breastplate. Something in him wanted to reach out and touch it, but he was afraid of the death with which it was in contact.

At long last he stood up. His legs were tingling from their overlong cramped position. He told himself that he had to get on with his journey. He was looking for live Spaniards. He did not need to waste more time with this dead one. As he turned to leave, he saw something on the ground a short distance away from the body. It was a long knife.

He walked over and bent to pick it up, but he hesitated. Again, he looked at the body. The long knife was not touching it. He told himself that it should be all right. He reached quickly, not allowing himself time to think further on it, and he grasped the long knife by its hilt and picked it up. It felt hard and cold. It was as long as his arm, and it was heavy. He held it out in front of himself, and the holding of it sent a thrill through his body. He smiled a broad smile, then turned and ran out of the building.

He had a weapon again, and not just any weapon. It was a Spanish long knife. It was—what had Deadwood Lighter called it?—*espada. La espada.* The sword.

'Squani almost left the town, feeling that he needed nothing more from it than the sword. But then he told himself that he should take the time to look further. He was still hungry, and he might find it difficult to hunt for meat with only the sword for a weapon. He found the town's storage house, but there was no grain left inside that was fit to eat. Then he made a systematic search of all the houses. When he was done, he had a bow and six arrows.

The bow needed to be restrung, but otherwise it seemed to be in fairly good shape. The feather fletching on the arrows was not in the best condition, but 'Squani thought that the arrows would fly anyway. They would have to do. But he would need to restring the bow.

He looked up into the sky and took note of the position

of the sun. She was well into the western half of the underside of the Sky Vault. Or, he corrected himself, it was low in the western sky. He had spent more time in the town than he realized. He decided that he would stay in the town for the night, taking the time to repair his newly acquired weapons and to find something to eat. He would start his journey again early the next morning.

He selected a house on the opposite side of town from the entryway, one that afforded him a good view of the rest of the area. It was in fair shape. He built a small fire just outside the door to the house. He put his bundle down beside the door, but he did not bother unrolling it. His small pouch of parched corn was empty, and there was nothing more in there that he would need for the night.

He wanted a good meal though, and he needed sinew with which to restring the bow. He decided to look first for food. He would be able to think better once he had eaten. The town's gardens had been long neglected, but perhaps something still grew there, something that would grow on its own without the constant attention of human beings. Taking up his sword, he headed for the garden plots.

The haft of the sword felt good in his hand, and the weight of the weapon was comforting to 'Squani. He swung it at his side as he walked, proud to have it in his possession. It was the weapon of the people of his father. Then 'Squani had an unsettling thought intrude in his mind. It occurred to him that he might actually be carrying his own father's weapon, that the hideous and neglected corpse in the townhouse could be that of his own father.

FOUR

'SQUANI was up and ready to travel early the next morning. Before retiring the night before, he had made a final search of the town. This time he had been more careful and much more thorough. He had found enough edible plants to satisfy his hunger, and he had located some abandoned deer sinew in one of the houses. It wasn't the best, but it would do until he could make a kill and replace it with new material. He was refreshed and again armed. He still had his own flint knife. Once again he had a bow and a few arrows, and he had *la espada,* the sword, the Spanish long knife, the weapon that could have, he kept telling himself, belonged to his own father.

He left the town and started walking along the road again, and he noticed that the landscape around him had changed. It had been a gradual change, of course, but he had not really noticed it before. He was almost out of the mountains, and before him stretched a vast, rolling plain. The river was still off to his left side, north of the road on which he traveled. At first he thought only about the difference in the countryside from the land to which he was accustomed. It was interesting to see the nearly flat, nearly treeless land. But then he started to get a little nervous again.

If someone should come along, he asked himself, where would he hide? Suddenly he felt very vulnerable, very much exposed. He turned around in the road and looked back behind himself. He looked in all directions. He saw no one, but he resolved to stay alert, to keep looking around himself to all sides to make sure that no one would slip up on him. Then he looked again toward the river.

There was a deer, a young stag. It was moving through the deep grass on its way to the river for a drink. 'Squani wondered how he could possibly have missed seeing it before. Yet it was there on the same side of the river as was he. He eased the burden off his back and dropped it quietly to the ground just beside the road. He put the precious sword down carefully on top of the bundle, and then he selected the best-looking of his recently acquired arrows and nocked it. He started inching toward the river.

He noticed, with silent thanks, that the wind was blowing in his direction, and it was not strong enough to interfere with his bow shot. A little closer, he moved on in a crouch. If he wasn't careful, he knew, the buck would become aware of his presence and spring away before he could get close enough for a good shot. He hesitated a moment, gauging the distance. He would have to get closer yet.

He got down on all fours and crept forward. At the river the deer drank, raised its head and looked around. Then it drank again. 'Squani crawled closer. Then when he knew he was close enough, he stood, pulled the bow and released the arrow. The shot was true. The buck jerked up, started to turn, then collapsed. 'Squani ran toward his kill, pulling out the flint knife as he ran.

Trotting Wolf, from his place high above the road, saw the people coming. He motioned to his two companions, and they ran to his side.

"What will we do?" asked He-Kills-Quickly. "They're not white people."

"They don't look like they could do us any harm," said the Howler. "They look helpless to me. They look ready almost to collapse in their tracks."

"Let's go down to the road and talk with them," said Trotting Wolf. "I'll step out to meet them. You two stay hidden and wait to see what happens."

"Howa," said the Howler.

"I'll find out who they are and where they're going," said Trotting Wolf. "Then we'll decide what to do."

The wretched people stopped walking when they saw the defiant figure of Trotting Wolf standing there in the middle of the road. An old woman moved close to an old man and spoke something in his ear. The old man stepped forward, ahead of the rest.

"My name is He-Kills-Many-Enemies," he said, speaking in the trade language common to the region, "but I suppose it should be changed now to He-Killed-Many-Enemies-Once-Years-Ago-When-He-Was-Young. I and these others with me are what is left of a town to the south and east of here. We are Cusabo People. Do you understand me? Do you know the trade language?"

"I understand you," said Trotting Wolf.

"Ah, good," said the old Cusabo man. "Are you Chalakee?"

"I am. I'm called Trotting Wolf, and I am a Wolf Person. You are entering the land of the Chalakee People."

Trotting Wolf used the jargon word, "Chalakee," for the Real People, as had the old man.

"Are we not welcome?" asked the old man.

"Because of the white men," said Trotting Wolf, "my people have decided to keep all outsiders away from our country."

"It's because of those same white men that we have become wandering refugees," said He-Kills-Many-Ene-mies. "Look at us. There are not enough of us to start a new town. We fought the white men twice, and this is what's left of us. We can no longer protect ourselves. We've gone to other towns of our own people and found them abandoned. Will you make us turn back again?"

Trotting Wolf thought for a moment. He felt pity for these wandering people, who were in this suffering condi-tion because of the very Spaniards he was on guard against. He thought also about the wish of High Back. Then he motioned for his two companions to come out of hiding and join him there in the road.

"Did you hear what the old man said?" he asked.

"Yes," said the Howler. "We heard. What will we do with these people?"

"I think that I'll tell them that it will be all right for them to camp over there by the side of the river for now," said Trotting Wolf. "Even if they have to move on, they need to rest first. You two keep watch as before. I'm going into Kituwah and talk with the people to see what they want to do about this."

He took a last look at the pitiful group there in the road. He remembered the resolution that he had helped to make, to keep all strangers out of the country of the Real People. But they had been thinking about the white people. They had not been thinking about people like these, people in need of help because of those very same white people. He hoped that the people of Kituwah would feel as he did and take pity on these refugees. And he regretted a little the wording of the resolution.

It was late evening. Soon the sun would crawl underneath the western edge of the Sky Vault, and the world would be dark until she reemerged on the eastern side in the morning. "No," 'Squani chastised himself. "Soon the sun will go down in the west, and it will be dark until it comes up again in the east. I must watch my thinking."

He sat beside the river near the spot where he had killed the deer. He had built a small fire, and he had eaten well, the first fresh meat he had tasted since leaving home. And there was plenty left. He also had a new bowstring made from the sinew of the deer.

He lounged back against the trunk of a lone tree, and he held the Spanish sword in his right hand, turning it this way and that, feeling its weight, admiring the glint of the shiny metal in the flickering light of the campfire.

"Espada," he said aloud, and then, *"Asquani."*

And he realized that for the first time in his life he was actually proud of his name. *Asquani.* Spaniard. He reaffirmed his resolve to do everything he could to live up to his name. He would become a Spaniard in more than name. He would become a Spaniard in every way: name, language, clothing, manners, beliefs, place of abode.

Finally he lay down to sleep. His mind was still racing, but he knew that he needed his sleep to continue the journey, and he was anxious to be up and on his way with the first light. As he drifted off to sleep, he still clutched the haft of the Spanish sword.

He came awake with a start. He had slept too late. It was

bright morning, but that was not the worst. There was a man standing over him. He had allowed someone to walk right up to him as he slept. He felt foolish and a little frightened. The man spoke to him, but 'Squani did not understand the words. Then he noticed that there were others behind the man, and they had hairy faces and strange clothing.

Spaniards, he thought with excitement. He thought about speaking to them in Spanish, but in his excitement, the words would not come to him. He decided to try the trade language on the brown-skinned one who had spoken to him.

"I don't understand your language," he said.

"Ah," said the other, also shifting to the jargon, "I thought that you might not be from this country. You are a traveler. Where do you come from?"

"I come from the land of the Chalakee," said 'Squani.

The other turned and spoke briefly to one of the white men, and 'Squani was startled to find that they did not speak Spanish. He did not know what language they were speaking. He felt a moment of panic. Surely these white men were Spaniards, but why were they not speaking their own language? Then the brown-skinned man turned back toward him and spoke again in the trade language.

"My friends are glad to hear that you're from the country of the Chalakee," he said. "They're looking for new people with whom to trade, and they would like to meet the Chalakees. Maybe you could help them."

"I don't think so," said 'Squani. "I'm traveling east. And besides, just before I left, the Chalakees decided to keep all strangers out of their land. If you try to go in there, you might be killed. But who are these men you're traveling with?"

"They're Frenchmen," said the other.

'Squani's brow wrinkled, and the other smiled.

"I bet you were thinking that they were Spaniards," he said. "The Spaniards are probably the only white men that the Chalakees have seen. But there are other white men. Just as there are different tribes of brown-skinned people, there are different tribes of white men. These Frenchmen are enemies of the Spaniards. You have nothing to fear from them. They are here as friends. They come to trade, not to steal and kill."

"Frenchmen," said 'Squani. He was glad that he had not spoken Spanish to these men. If they were enemies of the Spanish, they might have killed him. "Well," he said, "I'm not really a Chalakee. My mother is a Timucua woman from far south of here. Why don't you and your friends sit down while I build up my fire? I have fresh meat here. Plenty for all of us."

The other man spoke again to the Frenchmen, and one of them gave a brief answer. The man then faced 'Squani once more.

"Thank you," he said. "We will."

The brown-skinned man and his six white traveling companions sat around the embers of 'Squani's fire while 'Squani gathered up some more sticks. 'Squani soon had the fire going again, and he spitted some strips of venison over it to warm. He had cooked them the night before. Soon everyone had eaten his fill and quenched his thirst from the fresh running water of the river.

"My friend," said the brown-skinned man, apparently a

guide for the Frenchmen, "what are you called?"

'Squani had another moment of panic. His very name would give him away as an enemy of these white men. Or would it?

"I'm called Asquani," he said. "It's what the Chalakees call a Spaniard. My mother was a captive of the Spaniards for a time, and I'm a result of their use of her. She later became the wife of a Chalakee man, and they raised me there among his people to hate the Spaniards. Even so, they call me Asquani, Spaniard."

He had told nothing but the truth, but he had told it in such a way as to allow them to assume that he, too, hated Spaniards.

"My name is Little Black Bear," said the guide. "I'm a Catawba. These Frenchmen are the guests of my people. We've been trading with them. They're out looking for new trading partners, but they're also scouting for Spaniards, their enemies, and their enemies are also the enemies of my people."

"The Chalakees," said 'Squani, picking his words very carefully, "also consider the Spaniards to be their ene-mies." He picked up his Spanish sword by its haft and bal-anced it before him suggestively. "I, too, am looking for Spaniards."

Little Black Bear then spoke to the Frenchmen in what 'Squani assumed to be their language. He was probably telling them what 'Squani had said. Some of the Frenchmen responded. In a moment the conversation was over. One of the Frenchmen stood up and stepped toward 'Squani, holding out his hand. 'Squani stood, laying aside his sword, and took the hand.

"Asquani," said the Frenchman, *"je m'appelle Jacques Tournier."*

"His name is Jacques Tournier," said Little Black Bear.

'Squani nodded, and Tournier spoke some more French to him. 'Squani looked toward Little Black Bear for a translation.

"Jacques Tournier thanks you for your hospitality," said the Catawba guide. "He says that we won't go to the land of the Chalakees after what you have told us. We'll be going on our way. We may try to visit the Shawnees. He wishes you luck on your hunt, and he says that if you find any Spaniards and if you need any help, you can look for him or any of his French friends at my town. That's where they're staying. My town is called the Valley Town of the Catawbas. Ask anyone in Catawba country how to find it. Use my name. You'll be welcome there."

'Squani felt a great sense of relief when Little Black Bear and the Frenchmen had gone. So they wanted to kill Spaniards, he said to himself. Well, perhaps after he had found the Spaniards, he would tell them where they could find these Frenchmen, their enemies. Perhaps the Frenchmen would be the ones who would die.

FIVE

TROTTING WOLF went directly to the townhouse upon his arrival in Kituwah. It was late, and there were but a few men still there, smoking and visiting. One of them was the old man Dancing Rabbit. Trotting Wolf knew that Dancing Rabbit had been a *Kutani* years before, but that was all in the past. He knew the man and liked him well enough. He walked directly over to where Dancing Rabbit sat.

" *'Siyo,* my friend," he said.

" *'Siyo,* " said Dancing Rabbit. "I thought that you were gone to the mountain pass."

"I went out to the pass," said Trotting Wolf, "but there are some things happening out there that I alone can't make decisions about."

Dancing Rabbit gave Trotting Wolf a brief, curious look.

"What kinds of things?" he asked. "Can I be of any help to you?"

"I don't know," said Trotting Wolf with a shrug. "First, my clan brothers, the ones I went out there to relieve of their duties, said that they saw 'Squani going east on the road. I told them to tell his parents about that."

"Yes," said Dancing Rabbit. "I know about that already. They've been here, and they told Carrier, my nephew, and his wife."

"Did they know that he was going?"

"No. He left in the night without telling anyone. We're all worried about him, naturally, but what can we do? Should we try to chase him down and bring him back?"

Trotting Wolf gave another shrug.

"If a young man decides to leave, he leaves," he said. "When he's done what he set out to do, he'll come home."

"Yes," said Dancing Rabbit. "I suppose he will." But his brow was wrinkled with worry. "Unless he runs into some trouble he can't handle alone. But there's more?"

"Yes. A group of Cusabos came along the road heading this way. We stopped them, He-Kills-Quickly, the Howler and I. They're a pitiful group of refugees. They said that the Spaniards have attacked them twice, and other of their villages have been attacked. They're wandering and homeless. There are old ones and little children among them. I told them they could rest awhile there by the river."

"What's the problem then?" asked Dancing Rabbit.

"We resolved here to turn away all outsiders," said Trotting Wolf. "According to our resolution, I should turn these people away. But they're desperate. They're in need of help. They need food and clothes and shelter. And it was the white people who did this to them, the same white people who prompted our own resolution. My heart wants to take in these poor wanderers. It hurts me to see little ones suffering so."

"I don't see how you can allow them in without calling another meeting of the people," said Dancing Rabbit. "You yourself proposed the words: 'No one will be allowed in except Real People.'"

"Yes," said Trotting Wolf, pacing irritably. "I know, and I regret the words now. I should have proposed more flexible language. Perhaps I should have said— I don't know what."

"Well," said Dancing Rabbit, scratching his head, "we could call all the people together again, I suppose. That would take some time."

"Yes," said Trotting Wolf, "or . . ."

Dancing Rabbit waited a polite moment before speaking.

"Or what?" he asked.

"Or maybe there's some other way. Some way we could let them in right now that wouldn't violate the resolution."

"Well," said Dancing Rabbit, speaking slowly and

choosing his words carefully, "you could make them into Real People by adoption into your clan. You could make them Wolf People, and give them the responsibilities of Wolf People, and then they would be Real People. Then they could come in and be welcome. They would no longer be outsiders. The resolution would no longer apply. Of course, you may not want to take them into your clan. I don't know."

Trotting Wolf was listening intently, but he did not immediately answer. Dancing Rabbit furrowed his brow and thought for a while in silence. Then he continued.

"Yes," he said, nodding his head. "I suppose you could do it that way if you wanted to. That way it would be a clan matter, and once it was done, no one else would have anything to say about it."

Trotting Wolf smiled a smug, self-satisfied smile and nodded his head in agreement.

"Then that's the way it will be done," he said. He slapped Dancing Rabbit on the shoulder. "Thank you for your counsel, my friend."

"You should probably talk to others of your people," said Dancing Rabbit, "to other Wolf People, I mean. Especially to the women."

"Of course I'll do that," said Trotting Wolf, "but they'll take my advice on the matter, I think. They usually do. I'll be bringing the new Wolf People into town soon. Will you ask the people to prepare some food for them and some places for them to sleep?"

"Yes," said Dancing Rabbit. "Of course I will."

Trotting Wolf left the townhouse with a sense of accomplishment. He would go around to the homes of several of his clanswomen and get their assurances to back up his actions. Then he would go back out to the pass. Things would work out the way he wanted them to, he was confident, and then he would have accomplished two purposes. He would have taken in the refugees, as he wanted to do, and he would have increased the ranks of the Wolf Clan in order to make their task of guarding the passes a little easier. And he had even managed to get the suggestion for his action to come from someone else's mouth. He felt good.

Dancing Rabbit left the townhouse right behind Trotting Wolf, and he went first to the home of his nephew's wife, Potmaker, the Timucua woman. He found them still awake, sitting in front of the house. A small fire burned there between them. Potmaker went inside and returned almost immediately with a bowl of *kanohenuh* which she handed Dancing Rabbit.

"Wado," he said, and he tipped it up to his lips to drink.

"Uncle," said Carrier, "this has been a night for news."

Dancing Rabbit lowered the bowl and took a deep breath. Evidence of his long drink showed above his upper lip.

"Oh?" he said. He licked his upper lip to clean it off.

"Yes. First we had some bad news. The news that our son has left town."

"Yes," said Dancing Rabbit. "I know about that, of course."

"But we've had some good news too," said Carrier. "Potmaker just told me." He glanced at his wife. She smiled and ducked her head. Carrier grinned broadly. "She has a little one growing in her belly."

42

"An *usti?*" said Dancing Rabbit. "After all these years? That is good news. It makes me happy for you. For both of you.

"But nephew, we'll have to do something about finding a clan to adopt your wife. It should have been done long before this. I don't know why it hasn't been done. I suppose no one thought about it, or no one thought that it was urgent. But now you have a new one coming, something should be done. The *usti* will need a clan."

"Yes," said Carrier. "I think that something should be done about that."

He reached out and put an arm around the shoulders of his wife, and she looked down at the ground. She said nothing. It was not her place, she thought, to urge her own adoption into a clan. If they wanted her, they would invite her, she thought. In the meantime, she had her husband and her son. She would have the new one. Life went on.

"There's other business tonight," said Dancing Rabbit. "Trotting Wolf is bringing in a band of refugees. Cusabos, he said. To get around the recent resolution, he's adopting them into the Wolf Clan. They're tired and hungry, he said."

"And he's bringing them in tonight?" asked Carrier.

"Yes."

"I'll prepare some food," said Potmaker.

"Good," said Dancing Rabbit. "I have to go now and tell some others."

He stood up and started to walk away, but after a couple of steps, he stopped and turned to face them once again. He smiled a broad smile.

"I'm happy about the *usti,*" he said, "and try not to worry about 'Squani. I think he'll be all right. He'll come home again."

'Squani had spent another day traveling since the morning he had met the Frenchmen, and he had made himself another camp beside the same river. The day had been uneventful after the departure of the Frenchmen, and for that he was thankful. He had not found another village. He had not met any other travelers. He had been watchful, but he had not been able to keep the Frenchmen off his mind.

They were white men, like the Spaniards, but they were, according to the words of their own guide, enemies of the Spaniards. Everything 'Squani had heard about the Spaniards indicated that they were cruel, harsh and arrogant. But these other white men, these Frenchmen, had been friendly enough. Even when he had refused to take them into the country of the Real People, they had not gotten angry with him. They had not insisted. They had not threatened him. They had simply accepted his refusal. That was not the kind of behavior he had been led to expect from white men, at least not from Spaniards.

Of course, he had not told these Frenchmen of his intention to join the Spaniards, their enemies. He had not told them that he intended to become himself a full Spaniard, Spanish in every way. He had not told them that he was even considering telling the Spaniards about their presence in this country. Had he told them those things, they would undoubtedly have behaved in a very different way toward him.

He tried to force thoughts about the Frenchmen out of his mind and to think instead about the Spaniards. What would it be like, he wondered, to live with them? He thought about being surrounded constantly by only Spaniards, about speaking only Spanish, about relearning everything he thought he knew about the world. It was exciting to think about, but it was also a little frightening. With these thoughts swirling in his head, 'Squani drifted into sleep. The Spanish sword lay close by his side.

Little Black Bear had led Jacques Tournier and the other Frenchmen north after their meeting with 'Squani. They had made themselves a camp for the night beside a clear, running stream. They had eaten, and some of them were already stretched out on their blankets, settled in for the night. Little Black Bear stood a few feet away from the campfire staring into the darkness toward the north. Tournier walked over to stand beside him.

"Are you charting our journey for tomorrow, my friend?" asked Tournier.

"Oui," answered Little Black Bear, "in my mind."

Tournier was smoking a long, slender clay pipe, a habit he had quickly picked up in this land which was to him both new and strange.

"Tell me, *mon ami,*" he said, "this man we met, the lone traveler, the *indien* who calls himself Espagnol, what was the name of his people? Chalaque?"

Tournier had given a French pronunciation to the jargon word he had heard used for the Real People.

"Yes," said Little Black Bear, "Chalakee."

"Tell me about these Chalaques."

"Well," said the guide, "there are many of them, and they are powerful. They hold much land, mostly in the mountains. They have fifty or sixty towns, maybe more, very widespread. Many of the surrounding peoples have tried to take their territory."

"But without success?"

"Yes. Without success."

"Who is their chief?" asked the Frenchman.

"There is no big chief over all of the Chalakees," Little Black Bear answered. "Each town has its own chiefs. Two, I think. One for war and one for peace. Each town acts independently of the others, unless, of course, they all agree to cooperate in some action."

Tournier rubbed his chin and thought for a moment.

"Such as," he said, "a decision to keep all strangers out of their land?"

"Exactement," said the guide.

"Yes, I see," said Tournier. "Well, perhaps now is not quite the time, but one day soon, I think we will want to meet with these Chalaques. We will certainly want to make friends with them before the Spanish do."

"I think," said Little Black Bear, "that the Spanish will not make friends with the Chalakees. The Spanish have not made any real friends in this land. They don't try to make friends. They try to make slaves. And the Chalakees have already determined to keep the Spanish out of their country."

"According to the *indien* called Espagnol," said Tournier, "they have determined to keep *all* outsiders away."

"Yes, but because of the Spanish. Don't worry about the Spanish making friends with the Chalakees. That will never happen."

"I hope that you're right about that, *mon ami,* and you probably are, but we must make absolutely sure of it. We can't afford to take a chance on the Spanish making an ally here in the New World of such a powerful people as you say these Chalaques are. We cannot allow that to happen."

"So what will you do? They won't let us come into their country."

"If they won't let anyone come in, then they must send out their own traders sometime," said Tournier. "They can't exist in complete isolation, can they? Are they totally self-sufficient?"

"There have always been Chalakee traders, but I don't know what they're doing lately, since they've closed their borders. I suppose they'll have to come out to trade sooner or later. I don't know."

"Well then," said Tournier, "perhaps we will make our visit with the Shawnees a quick one. Then perhaps we should come back this way and see if we can pick up the trail of our friend, the Espagnol. Let's see if he finds the Spaniards he's looking for and see what happens if he does find them. Something may develop from that. What do you think, *mon ami?*"

Little Black Bear shrugged.

"Cela se peut," he said. It may.

SIX

TROTTING WOLF led all the wretched Cusabo refugees into Kituwah, where many of the resident women had already prepared food. The poor wandering souls ate better than they had in many days, and

47

their children actually began to run and play with children of Kituwah. Trotting Wolf watched with great pleasure and satisfaction as the expressions on the Cusabo children's faces changed from sadness and misery to joy.

And the children were not the only ones whose looks betrayed their sense of relief. The lines that pain and worry had etched on the older ones were still there, but underneath the lines, the faces were relaxed. Everyone was well fed.

Trotting Wolf announced to the people of Kituwah that all of the men in this wandering group of Cusabos had been adopted into the Wolf Clan of the Real People. If the men had wives, of course, those women would have to be adopted into other clans, and other family relationships had to be considered as well. But if there were no other family complications, then unmarried women, or widowed women with children, were also made Wolves.

The Wolf Clan of the Real People was considerably strengthened by this action, and Trotting Wolf explained to the Cusabos, the newly made Real People, that as Wolves, they would share the responsibility of guarding the passes to keep outsiders out of the country of the Real People. He assured them, of course, that they would be given plenty of time to rest and regain their strength. All of them readily agreed to this bargain. They were happy to have a place to stay where they would be safe and well fed.

Dancing Rabbit watched the welcoming festivities with interest. He took the time to meet most of the new Wolf People and chat a little with them, and he spent some time in conversation with the old man He-Kills-Many-Enemies. He found the old man easy to like. Dancing Rabbit knew that he had been manipulated by Trotting Wolf into making the suggestion to adopt these people, but it had all worked out well, and he was pleased. And he had known at the time that he was only making the suggestion that Trotting Wolf was looking for anyhow.

But there was something else on the mind of Dancing Rabbit. There was another matter of adoption with which he was concerned, and it seemed to him more and more as the evening wore on into night, that the time was right. The circumstances would never be better. He looked around for Trotting Wolf.

It wasn't hard to locate the man. Not only was he a striking figure, but he was a center of attention during these festivities. He was surrounded by members of his own clan, both old ones and the newly made ones. Dancing Rabbit sidled into the crowd to await his chance.

"This is a good feast," Trotting Wolf was saying, "but I've been absent from the mountain long enough. I've left only two men there to guard the pass. I have to go back now, but you new Wolf People, you'll be well taken care of here in Kituwah."

"My friend," said Dancing Rabbit, "I'd like a word with you before you go."

"Walk with me," said Trotting Wolf, and he headed for the passageway to leave the town. Dancing Rabbit fell in beside him, limping slightly from his old wound.

"You know my nephew," he said.

"Carrier?" said Trotting Wolf. "The one that used to go with you on your trading trips?"

"Yes. Carrier."

"He's the father of 'Squani," said Trotting Wolf. "The

one that was seen leaving here."

"Yes. He is. You know he found his wife far to the south of here. She's a Timucua woman. He rescued her from the *Ani-Asquani*."

"I remember the story."

"No one ever adopted Potmaker into a clan. Her son therefore has no clan. He was born here in Kituwah and raised here, yet he's not a Real Person."

Trotting Wolf walked on in silence, waiting to hear if Dancing Rabbit would say more. He had an idea that he knew what Dancing Rabbit wanted of him. Still, he waited.

"It's not good for a young man to be without a clan," Dancing Rabbit said, "and now Potmaker is going to have another *usti*. I hate to think that it, too, will grow up here without a clan. It's not good."

Trotting Wolf stopped walking and turned to face Dancing Rabbit. He looked Dancing Rabbit in the face only briefly, then put his hands on the shorter man's shoulders.

"You're right," he said. "Something should be done about that. I think probably something will be done very soon. We'll talk about this matter again, my friend, within four days."

Dancing Rabbit stood and watched as Trotting Wolf moved on toward the passageway out of town. He smiled. Nothing definite had been said, yet he had a feeling that his mission had been accomplished. Trotting Wolf had understood, and Trotting Wolf would almost certainly act. Potmaker would have a clan, and therefore her children would also have a clan. Everything would be all right.

. . .

Squani had lost track of the number of days and nights he had been traveling. He had not known, to begin with, how long a journey it would be, and did not know even yet just where he was going. He knew only that he had already made a long journey, and that the landscape around him had changed considerably. Most recently, he had noticed something in the air, a different smell or taste or—something. He wasn't at all sure what it was, but there was something different about the air. And, though he could not say why, he had a feeling that he must be getting near his final destination.

After the first several days of the journey, the initial excitement of his plans had given way to the tedium of travel. But with this new feeling, the excitement returned, and it was an even more intense excitement than before. The Spanish must be somewhere near, he told himself. He would find them. He would meet them, carrying his Spanish sword and speaking their language. And he could not imagine any reason why they would not welcome him with open arms as one of their own.

He continued east, and he found the charred remains of a village. He could not be sure whether there had been a fight there or not. There could be other explanations for a burned town. He walked on another day, and then he found another town. This one was still in good shape, but it had been abandoned. He found some useful items there: a few more good arrows, some robes, a better bow than the one he had been carrying. He looked for some kind of evidence to explain why the town had been abandoned, but he found none. He spent a night in the town and left early the next morning, his bundle bigger and heavier than it had been before. He still headed east.

He noticed that the river alongside of which he traveled had grown wider, but of more interest to him was the sight off in the east, of what appeared to be another forest. He had been in open prairie for some time. The thought of a cool forest with ample concealment was more than welcome. He hurried ahead, but by the day's end he had still not reached the trees. They did appear to be nearer, and he was at last sure that it was actually a forest for which he was headed. He slept the night in a small grove of trees beside the river.

The sun was directly overhead the next day when he came across another abandoned village. It was the fourth he had found so. There had to be a reason for it, and the unavoidable conclusion which came to his mind was that the empty villages were almost certainly evidence of Spanish activity along the same route which he traveled. He had heard the story of the De Soto expedition told by Deadwood Lighter. He had heard of the way in which the Spaniards had wiped out entire villages, and he had heard how many people, on learning of the approach of the Spaniards, simply fled, leaving everything behind them.

This thought gave him mixed feelings, for he did not like to dwell on the alleged cruelties of the Spaniards. On the other hand, if he was right about the reason for the empty towns, he was probably getting close to the Spaniards. His destination was near. He tried to concentrate on that happy thought.

The end of that day, he came at last to the edge of the

forest. It was thick with tall pines, not at all like the forests of his mountain home. He did not go on into the forest. He made his camp for the night there just at the edge and a bow shot north of the trail. As he drifted off to sleep, he listened to the strange sounds of unfamiliar night birds.

He slept well enough, and in the morning he had just rolled up his bundle and was getting ready to strike out again when he saw the three *Indios* walking along the trail. He had begun using the Spanish word to designate the brown-skinned people who were native to the land. It made him feel good. It separated him from them and associated him, at least in his own mind, with the Spaniards.

He left his bundle there on the ground and stood up, taking a couple of steps toward the trail.

"Hello," he shouted, using the trade language. "Do you understand me?"

The three travelers stopped and looked around. One of them pointed toward where 'Squani stood. Another had already nocked an arrow, but seeing that 'Squani seemed not at all threatening, he relaxed. The one who had pointed called out.

"Hello," he said. "Yes. We understand you."

'Squani left his belongings, all except the Spanish sword which he carried casually at his side, and walked toward the others. He waited until he had walked about half the distance between them before he spoke again.

"I'm a stranger here," he said.

"Where do you come from?" asked the spokesman for the travelers.

"From the country of the Chalakees. The last four towns I passed by were abandoned."

"Yes," said the man. "One of them was probably ours. Most of this country has been abandoned because of the Spanish nearby."

'Squani felt a thrill run through his body, but he suppressed it.

"Are they very near?" he asked. By this time he had reached the trail, and he stood close to the others. He noticed that they were looking at his sword.

"Are you looking for the Spaniards?" asked one of the men.

"Yes," said 'Squani. "I'm looking for them. I've been looking for a long time." He lifted the Spanish sword, not enough to make a threatening gesture, just enough to make it seem to imply something about his statement. The other three looked at it and then at each other. "And you?" he asked.

"We're looking for them too. We hope to catch one or two of them away from the rest. Without their big animals, the ones that they ride, you know?"

"Yes," said 'Squani. "I know about them."

"And without their vicious dogs. Is that what you plan to do? Hide in the woods and wait for them? You could join us."

"I heard that they were on an island in the big water," said 'Squani. "I want to go there."

"You want to go to the island? There are too many of them there. They'd kill you for sure. They'd kill you before you could kill even one of them. The dogs would get you."

"There are probably two hundred Spaniards on the island. Maybe more."

"That's where I want to go," said 'Squani. "Can you tell me how to get there?"

The three looked at one another again. Then one shrugged.

"We can take you to it," he said. "If that's what you really want to do. We can take you through the woods and show it to you, but we won't go to the island with you."

"That's all right," said 'Squani. "I want to go to the island of the Spaniards alone. If you show me how to get there, that's all I want."

"Then let's go."

"I have some things over there. Let me get them, and then I'll follow you."

'Squani turned and trotted toward his campsite where he had left his belongings. His new acquaintances watched him from the trail.

"Is he crazy, this Chalakee?" asked one.

"I don't know," said another. "It seems so, but I don't know."

SEVEN

CAPITÁN MARCOS ZAVALA sat in the rude hut that he called his office. He sat in a chair constructed of native wood by slave labor, behind a table of the same make, and he wrote in his journal with a native quill. He did not know the name of the bird from which the quill had been acquired. He was beginning to believe that the governor had punished him with this assignment. Others conquered empires and searched for gold. Zavala had been told to occupy this wretched island and to build a permanent outpost there for Spain. The only building material available was wood, and the weather was wet. His hastily constructed hut leaked, and his work was all tedium.

"*Capitán?*"

Zavala looked up from his writing to see the head of Félix Ocampo, his trusted lieutenant, poking into the doorway.

"What is it, Félix?" he asked.

"Excuse the interruption, *Capitán,*" said Ocampo, "but it's the priest again."

"What does he want now?" said Zavala, the irritation he felt evident in his voice. He laid aside his quill and leaned back in his chair.

"I don't know, *Capitán.* The same old thing, I suppose. He's demanding to see you."

"Well, let him come in."

That was the other reason Zavala had decided that he was being punished. The governor had insisted that he take along the priest, Father Tomás Lucero, and he had further insisted that Zavala cooperate with Father Tomás.

"Capitán Zavala," said the priest, stepping into the office.

"*Sí, sí, padre,*" said Zavala. "Come in. Come in and have a seat. Will you have a glass of wine with me?"

"No, thank you," said the priest. He sat in a chair much like the one in which Zavala sat. It was not directly across the table from Zavala. Rather, it sat against the far wall in the small room. Father Tomás sat stiffly, his hands folded in his lap.

"Well, I'm sure you'll forgive me if I have one," said Zavala. He reached to the far corner of the table for a glass and a bottle, and he poured the glass full of red wine. "What can I do for you?"

"Not for me," said Father Tomás. "For the Church. For your God."

"I'm a soldier, *padre,*" said Zavala. He took a sip from his wineglass. "I leave doing for God up to you and your kind."

"You have your orders, Capitán. You were told to cooperate with me fully, I believe. If you fail to do so, I will be forced to report that failure upon my return to Spain."

"*Padre,* I'm sure that when you get back to Spain, there will be no end of complaints regarding my behavior. In the meantime, don't threaten me. Just tell me, what is your complaint, and then leave me alone."

Father Tomás stiffened even more, and his face turned red in attempting to control his anger.

"Where is my congregation?" he asked. "When am I to be allowed to fulfill the task for which I was sent here? By royal command, I was sent here charged with saving souls. I must be allowed to pursue that end."

"*Padre,* we have one hundred *Indios* here on this island. How many of them have you brought into your flock, huh? How many Christians have you made of our one hundred savages? Make one hundred Christians here, on this island, and I promise you that I'll gather up some more heathens for you to preach to."

"How can I preach to men you're working to death? By the time I'm allowed to gather them together, they're exhausted. They can hardly stay awake. Some of them are dying. They don't understand Spanish. You don't give me time to teach them.

"How can I preach to women you and your men are debauching for your own pleasure? How can I speak of the sins of the flesh?"

Zavala smashed a fist down on the table and stood up from his chair.

"I don't know how, *padre*," he said. "That's *your* job. You figure out how to preach. Don't ask me. And as for the men being on the verge of death, that should be the best time for you to save a soul. Promise them a path to heaven."

"I spoke of heaven to one of the men," said the priest. "He asked me if Capitán Zavala would be there. I told him, perhaps wrongly, that you would be—eventually. Do you know what he said to that?"

Zavala laughed. "He probably said that he didn't want to go if he would see me up there."

"You find that amusing? Take care of your own soul, *Capitán,* or you may find yourself in hell."

"Then the joke will be on the savage," said Zavala. "He'll meet me after death anyhow. Now leave me. I have work to do, and I'm tired of your whining and your preaching."

"*Capitán—*"

"Félix," roared the captain.

Félix Ocampo hurried into the room and stood at attention.

"*Sí, Capitán?*"

"Father Tomás is leaving," said Zavala. "Will you escort him out?"

Father Tomás stood up from his chair and glared at Zavala for a moment.

"That won't be necessary, Félix," he said, and he turned and left the room.

Zavala poured himself another glass of wine.

"God save me," he said, "from a god damned priest."

'Squani's main guide moved slowly through the trees. We must be getting close, 'Squani thought. Then the man stopped and held up his hand as a signal to the others. He stood quietly for a moment, then looked over his shoulder and motioned for 'Squani to move up beside him. 'Squani did so, keeping as quiet as he could. His guide was pointing straight ahead. 'Squani looked, and the sight he saw amazed him.

Never before had he seen so much water. He thought for a moment that he was actually standing on the edge of the world. There was nothing but water for as far as he could see. Off to his right a narrow peninsula shot out into the vast water, and off the far end of the peninsula was a long, narrow, thickly wooded island. The woods, however, seemed to have been stripped from the edge of the island.

"They are there," said his guide. "On the island. You can see where they cut down the trees."

"Why did they do that?" asked 'Squani.

"I think so they can see if anyone is coming. Also, they used the trees to build their houses. The houses are hidden from our view here by trees that are still standing, but they're in there. The Spaniards are in there. Are you really going in there alone?"

"Yes. That's what I've come here for," said 'Squani. "Thank you for showing me the way."

"Then we'll part company here," said the other. "We're

not going on the island."

'Squani stood alone while the other three men vanished back into the darkness of the woods. He stared toward the dark island, the island covered with tall trees which hid the houses of the Spaniards. His journey was over, but his new life, he told himself, was just about to begin. The island was just there, in his sight. So what was he waiting for?

His heart was beating fast, and he was sweating. How would he get to the island? Swim? Would he just boldly walk up to the Spaniards? What would they do when they saw him? Would they shoot before he had a chance to talk to them? There were *Indios* in these woods waiting to attack unsuspecting Spaniards. He had just met three of them. The Spaniards must know of them, and they might think that he was one of them.

He had not thought of these problems before, but with the island right there in front of him, the problems came to the front of his mind. He still wanted to meet the Spaniards. He wanted to live with them. He did not want to be killed by them. He sat down there at the edge of the woods and leaned back against a tree trunk to think. The sun was low in the western sky. It would not be wise to approach the Spanish island just before dark. He decided to sleep there in the woods for the night and make his approach in the morning. That would give him a night to think about just how to accomplish it. He would plan exactly what to say when first he saw a Spaniard. He would be fresh and alert. Yes, he thought. Morning would be better.

He unburdened his back and stretched himself out on the ground, resting his head on the pack. Soon he was asleep.

He was awakened by horrible, loud noises, noises that

seemed to come from another world. It was like *yansa,* buffalo, stamping the earth, but there were clanking sounds along with it, something like sheets of mica rattling together, but much louder and harder-sounding, and there was shouting along with the other sounds.

He was up on his hands and knees looking in the direction from which the sounds seemed to be coming, and then suddenly there was a new stamping and clanking and almost immediately a shout, and it was all right behind him, on top of him. He spun and looked up at the most frightful thing he had ever seen.

"Here's another one," he heard it say in the Spanish tongue.

He remembered his lessons with Deadwood Lighter, and his mind told him that it was nothing but a Spaniard mounted on the back of a *caballo,* but it was huge and it was stamping so near him that he was frightened nearly into speechlessness. The figure atop the *caballo* raised his right arm, and in it he held a sword. It was much like the one that 'Squani carried. Then 'Squani found his voice.

"Pare," he shouted. *"Por favor. Yo soy Español."*

The man lowered his sword and backed his horse away from 'Squani. He leaned forward and looked at 'Squani with wide eyes.

"You say you're Spanish?" he asked.

"Sí," said 'Squani. *"Español.* I've come here looking for you. Look. Look."

He reached carefully for his own Spanish sword and picked it up. Then he held it out for the other to see. The horseman sat up straight again, looked beyond 'Squani and shouted.

"Hey," he said. "Hey, come here. Come and see what I've found. Hurry."

Soon three other horsemen came riding up. 'Squani noticed right away that they were holding swords with bloody blades.

"We've killed three of them," one of the men said, "and you've found another?"

"Quién sabe?" said the man who had found 'Squani. "This one claims to be Spanish."

The others rode up close and looked down at 'Squani. 'Squani's heart still pounded, but he was not as afraid as before. He had actually conversed with a Spaniard. The man had been ready to kill him, but he had stopped when he heard 'Squani's words.

"Look at him," said one of the newcomers. "He claims to be Spanish? Does he take us for fools?"

"He spoke to me in Spanish."

The skeptical newcomer looked at 'Squani intently for a moment. Then he swung one leg over the back of his horse and dropped heavily onto the ground with a clank. He took a couple of steps toward 'Squani, then stood with his hands on his hips.

"Stand up," he said.

'Squani stood.

"Look me in the face."

It was a difficult thing for 'Squani to do. All of his upbringing told him that it was rude, even threatening, to look another in the face, in the eyes, but that was what the man wanted. 'Squani looked him in the face. There wasn't much face to see. Most of it was covered by hair, bristly-looking hair. It was a light brown color streaked with gray.

"Me entiende usted?" the man asked.

"Sí, señor," said 'Squani.

"You speak Spanish?"

"Sí."

"Did I hear right a moment ago? Did you say you are Spanish?"

"Sí," said 'Squani. "My father is Spanish. I have come a long way to find you. I want to be with my father's people."

EIGHT

THE mounted men walked their horses, with 'Squani trotting along ahead of them. It took longer to get to the island than 'Squani thought it would. He tried to recall the details of what had just happened. The sun was out of sight, but it was not yet quite dark. He had decided to sleep in the woods and approach the island in the morning, but he must have fallen asleep almost immediately. Then the Spaniards had discovered him there. He remembered that they had said they had just killed three *Indios.* 'Squani figured that the unfortunate victims had probably been his former guides. He regretted that, but he reminded himself that those three had themselves been looking for Spaniards to kill.

They arrived at the end of the peninsula, and 'Squani stopped. The island was not far ahead, but there was water in between. He looked over his shoulder toward the Spanish horsemen.

"Go on," said one of the men. "It's not deep. Not just now."

Still 'Squani hesitated, and the horseman urged his mount ahead, riding past 'Squani and into the water.

"You see?" he said. "Come on."

'Squani waded into the water and followed the man. The other two riders came along behind. At its deepest point the water reached only to 'Squani's knees. Soon they were on the island. And soon, 'Squani thought, he would be a real Spaniard.

The horse and rider ahead of him moved up onto dry land, and 'Squani followed them. He was amazed at how easy it had been. He had expected to have to swim or even find himself a boat of some kind in order to get from the mainland to the island. It had never occurred to him that he would be able to walk to it.

They crossed the wide perimeter which the Spaniards had cleared of trees and moved onto a path cut into the woods. Tall pines towered above their heads, and the ground was darkened by their shade. With the light of the sun almost gone, 'Squani thought that it was dark indeed. Soon, however, he saw light coming from another source.

He followed the horseman ahead of him into a clearing in which the eerie light of several flickering fires lit the fronts of small log houses. Several men who were lounging about called out greetings to the new arrivals, and one man stepped out of one of the houses and shouted in a commanding voice.

"What have you got there?" he asked.

"Capitán," answered the rider who had led the way into the clearing, "we killed three who acted like they wanted to fight. Then we found this one. He claims to be a Spaniard, and he speaks Spanish."

"So we thought we'd bring him to you instead of killing him," said one of the riders behind 'Squani.

Capitán Zavala walked up very close to 'Squani and studied him intently for what seemed to 'Squani like a very long time.

"You speak Spanish, huh?"

"Sí, Capitán," said 'Squani. He was proud of himself for having taken note of the title by which the other man had addressed this one.

"You don't look like a Spaniard to me," said Zavala. He walked once around 'Squani and studied him some more. "It could be the clothes, though," he said, "and the way the hair is done. You don't really look *Indio* either. Where did you come from?"

"From west of here," said 'Squani. "From the land of the Chalaque." He used the Spanish pronunciation of the jargon word for the Real People. He had learned it from Deadwood Lighter. He had also noticed earlier, when he had met the Frenchmen, that the French pronunciation for the same word was very similar to the Spanish.

"You're a Chalaque?" said Zavala.

"No," said 'Squani. "My mother was a Timucua woman from Florida. My father was Spanish. But I was raised by the Chalaques."

"So where did you learn to speak Spanish?"

"We had among us an old man who had been a slave on the De Soto expedition. He had been among the Spaniards for a long time and knew their language well. He taught me."

"What is your name?" asked Zavala.

"The Chalaques call me Asquani. That's their way of

pronouncing the word Spaniard."

"Your name is Spaniard?"

"Sí, señor."

Zavala laughed, and he was joined almost immediately by the others. 'Squani wondered what was so funny to them about his name. After all, it was a name that identified him. He felt his face burning with embarrassment.

"To the Chalaques," he said, "it's an insult. They taunted me with it."

Zavala stopped laughing, and so did the others.

"And what is it to you, Spaniard?" asked the captain.

"I'm proud of my name and of my father. When I learned that there were Spaniards here, I left the Chalaques to find you. I want to stay here. My father was a Spaniard. I'm a Spaniard."

Zavala looked down at the sword in 'Squani's right hand.

"And where did you get that sword, Spaniard?" he asked.

"I found it in an abandoned village on my way here," said 'Squani.

"Well, perhaps I should keep it for you—for now."

'Squani hesitated. He hated to part with the sword, but he was with Spaniards. Perhaps he did not need the sword so much now anyway. He handed it to Zavala.

"Perhaps when I know you better," said the captain, "I'll return it to you. So, you want to be a real Spaniard, do you?"

"Sí, Capitán," said 'Squani. "That is what I want most of all. That's why I traveled so far."

"Well, I suppose you can stay with us. You can start by

earning to build houses the way we Spanish build them. That's what we're doing here. Building houses."

"I'll do anything," said 'Squani. "I want to learn."

"*Bueno,*" said Zavala. Then he turned his head slightly and called out over his shoulder. "Félix."

Félix Ocampo came running up to stand in front of the captain.

"*Sí, Capitán?*"

"Take this—Spaniard and show him where to sleep."

"Yes, *Capitán,*" said Ocampo, "but—where?"

"With the others, of course."

"Zavala!"

The new voice was loud, angry, almost threatening, and t was every bit as authoritative as that of the captain. 'Squani turned to look for its source, and he saw another Spaniard. This one, though, wore a long black robe. His face was stern, and he glared at Capitán Zavala.

"*Sí, Padre Tomás,*" said Zavala, his voice suddenly tired. "What can I do for you now?"

"You don't need this one as a slave. You have one hundred. This one speaks Spanish. He is half Spanish himself, if he speaks the truth. Give him to me."

Zavala smirked.

"For what?" he said.

"He wants to learn. He said so. Let me teach him. He will be my first convert, and because he is half *Indio,* he will help me to convert others. He can be invaluable."

Zavala looked at 'Squani again. Then he looked at the priest. Perhaps this gesture would be enough to keep Father Tomás off his back for a while. Yes. This mestizo could be a godsend. Zavala faced the priest and smiled. He bowed a gracious bow and made a sweeping gesture toward 'Squani.

"Father Tomás," he said, "I present him to you in the name of God and the Holy Church with the greatest of pleasure. Save his soul, by all means, and through him save a thousand. I wouldn't have it any other way."

The priest stepped over to 'Squani and looked him hard in the eyes. 'Squani tried to return the look, but he couldn't quite maintain the stare. He dropped his eyes to the ground.

"Of course," said Father Tomás, "you cannot be called Spaniard. That will never do. You must have a new name. You will be Fortunato, for among your kind, you are indeed fortunate. Come with me, Fortunato. You will eat and you will sleep, and in the morning we'll get you some proper clothing. Then your studies will begin."

The next weeks went quickly for 'Squani. Father Tomás told him stories from the Bible, the big book that Deadwood Lighter had told him about. 'Squani learned that God the Father created the world in six days and rested on the seventh. He learned about Adam and Eve, the first man and first woman, and how God placed them in the Garden of Eden where they had everything they needed in abundance until the serpent tempted Eve, and she in turn tempted Adam and made him eat the forbidden fruit of the Tree of Knowledge.

The story sounded remarkably similar, to 'Squani, to the story of Kanati and Selu, the Great Hunter and the Corn Mother. In the story told by the Real People, they were the first man and woman, and they, too, had everything they

68

needed and enjoyed a life of ease. And they had a son.

But then one day Selu washed some meat in the fresh stream near her house. Later she and her husband heard noises as if there were two boys at play. They asked their son later about the voices, and he told them that he had been playing with a little wild boy.

"Bring him home with you the next time you play with him," said Selu. "We want to meet him."

The next day they heard the voices again, but when their son came home, he was alone.

"Where's your friend?" asked Kanati.

"He said that you don't like him. He said he won't come here because you threw him away."

The next day Kanati followed his son secretly when the boy went out to play, and he saw his son meet the wild boy. He waited until the two boys were wrestling, and he ran out of hiding and caught the wild boy. The wild boy kicked and screamed, trying to get free of the grasp of Kanati.

"Let me go. Let me go. You threw me away."

But Kanati took him home to Selu, and they took care of him. He had grown in the river from the blood that Selu had washed off the meat. Kanati and Selu raised him as their own, but he stayed wild, and often he led his brother into mischief.

Whenever the family needed meat, Kanati would go into the woods and soon come back with a freshly killed deer. He never failed. One morning when they needed meat, the wild boy whispered to his brother.

"Let's follow our father and see where he gets that meat," he said. And so they did. They followed Kanati into the woods until he came to a huge rock which sealed the entrance to a cave. Kanati rolled the rock aside just a little and a deer sprang out of the cave into view. Quickly Kanat rolled the rock back into place, nocked an arrow and sho the deer.

"So that's how he does it," said the wild boy.

Kanati took the deer and started for home, and as soor as he was out of sight, the wild boy headed for the cave entrance.

"Come on," he said to his brother.

The two naughty boys pushed the rock aside, but it wa. so heavy that they couldn't put it back in place, and sud denly deer came running out, hundreds and hundreds of deer. They knocked the boys down and ran over them nearly trampling them to death. When the two bruised and scratched boys could finally sit up again, and the deer were all gone, Kanati came back, and he was very angry.

He went back inside the cave, and he found there an earthen pot with a lid on it. He kicked it over and broke it to pieces, and millions of stinging and biting bugs came flying out. They swarmed over the two boys, buzzing, biting, stinging. The boys screamed and slapped at the insects, and when the swarms had finally gone on, the boys were covered with sore and itching red bumps.

"From now on," said Kanati, "we'll have to work hard for our meat."

When 'Squani told this tale to Father Tomás, he thought that the priest would find its similarities to the story of the Garden of Eden as interesting as 'Squani had found them to be, but the priest turned angry instead.

"Forget that heathenish tale," he said. "It's blasphemy. The story I have told you is the one true story. All truth is in the Bible. Adam was the first man. No one else. And Eve was the first woman. There can be no other. They were tempted by the serpent, and their sons were Abel and Cain."

'Squani was a little frightened by the stern expression on the *padre*'s face and by the anger in his voice. He decided that he wouldn't bother to finish the story and tell Father Tomás about how the boys had watched their mother rubbing her belly to fill baskets with corn and beans, and how they had then decided that she was a witch. They killed her then, but before they did, she told them to drag her body in seven circles so that they would always have corn. It would grow in one night. The boys had gotten tired of dragging the body, and so, according to the tale, it now takes much longer to grow corn. Something told 'Squani that the *padre* would really get angry with part of the tale, so he kept quiet.

"Do you understand me, Fortunato?"

"*Sí, padre,*" 'Squani said. "I will forget that story."

NINE

PERHAPS it was because things had been so quiet. There had been no attempts by anyone to get into the country of the Real People. The Wolves continued to guard the passes, but Trotting Wolf worried that the people might begin to think he and his clan brothers were engaged in foolishness. He thought that the people needed something to remind them that what the Wolf Clan was doing was really important.

And so he decided to send out the scouts. They would

wander the surrounding countryside for any signs of the white men, and then they would report back to Trotting Wolf. If he could provide evidence that the dangerous white men were still in the vicinity, the people would know how important it was that the Wolves guard the passes.

Trotting Wolf was more than a little surprised, though, when the young man called Breath, a Cusabo, one of the newly made Wolves, returned so soon.

Trotting Wolf himself was watching the pass when Breath came walking down the road headed for Kituwah. As soon as he recognized the young man, Trotting Wolf started down the mountainside toward the road.

"Breath," he called out.

Breath stopped and looked in the direction of the voice.

" *'Siyo,* Trotting Wolf," he said.

"You're back much sooner than I expected," said Trotting Wolf.

"I have news. I thought that you'd want to hear it."

"Yes," said Trotting Wolf. "Of course."

"There are white men not far from here. Six of them. They're being guided by a Catawba man from the Valley Town of the Catawbas, and they've been to visit the Shawnee People."

"Only six white men?" said Trotting Wolf.

"Yes."

"That seems strange. They must be scouts for a larger party."

"I don't think so," said Breath. "I talked to some Shawnees after the white men had left. These were not *Ani-Asquani.* They were a different tribe of white men, enemies of the *Ani-Asquani.* The Shawnees told me that these white men aren't searching for yellow metal or catching slaves. They're staying at the Valley Town of the Catawbas. They sent out these six to try to establish trade relations with people here."

"If they're trying to start trade," said Trotting Wolf, "I wonder why they didn't come to see us."

"The Shawnee said that these men had heard about what we're doing here. That's why they didn't come to see us."

Trotting Wolf felt a little slighted. If these new white people were just trying to get acquainted in the area, trying to establish trade relations, they should have made an attempt to meet with the Real People, the most powerful people in all the area. Still it was good to know that the word had spread about the Wolf Clan, and that these new white people were afraid to challenge their authority.

"Good," he said. "Good. You go on into town now. Get some food and rest. You've done well."

As he watched Breath moving along the road, Trotting Wolf considered these new developments. So the white men, like the brown-skinned people, existed in different tribes. And now there were two tribes of them in the vicinity, and the two were enemies. Well, good, he thought. Maybe they would have a war and kill each other off.

But if one side should win a clear victory, Trotting Wolf hoped that the losers would be the *Ani-'squani.* Apparently these new ones were not so brutal. Perhaps, he thought, perhaps the Real People should become involved in this war on the side of the new white men. Maybe together they could drive the *Ani-Asquani* away or wipe them out completely.

But then, how could they be sure that these new ones were not really as bad as the others? Perhaps with their enemies out of the way, they would show their true nature. No, he decided. The Real People had been right in the first place to isolate themselves from all outside events and to keep all strangers out of their country. That was still the best policy. They would wait and see what happened when the two white enemies came face to face.

As Father Tomás continued his Bible tales, 'Squani was continually struck with the similarities between those tales and the ones told by the Real People. He heard the story of Cain and Abel, and he was again reminded of Selu. Hers was also a story of the first death in the world. Of course, he did not mention this comparison to Father Tomás.

He was also interested in hearing that when Cain went out from the Garden, he went to the Land of Nod and found himself a wife. After that, Father Tomás told 'Squani how the descendants of Adam and Eve grew into the tribes of Israel, people that the priest called Jews. 'Squani took all that in easily enough until Father Tomás told him that all of humanity was descended from Adam and Eve.

Up until then, 'Squani had taken the tales the same way he had always taken those of the Real People. The Real People had their stories. The *Ani-Cusa* had theirs, and the *Ani-Tsiksa* theirs. None of them took into account the origins of other tribes of people, so 'Squani easily accepted Father Tomás's tales as the story of the origin of the people called Jews.

But Father Tomás insisted that his Bible told the story of

the origin of *all* people. That troubled 'Squani. It made no sense to him.

"Pardon me, Father," he said. "Are the Spaniards Jews?"

"No," said Father Tomás, and he seemed a little angry at the question. "Of course not."

The priest's facial expression and tone of voice prompted 'Squani to keep further questions and doubts to himself, but still he wondered. Why was Father Tomás telling him stories of the origin of the Jews, telling him that all truth was in the big book he carried, which was the book of the stories of the Jews, insisting that all people came from the union of Adam and Eve, and then saying that he himself was not a Jew?

There was much that 'Squani did not, could not understand, but he at last decided to keep quiet in the future. His questions only seemed to anger the priest. So he would ask no more questions. He reminded himself that he had made up his mind to become a real Spaniard. He would try to be patient. He would keep quiet, pay attention and learn.

There was one thing, though, about which he found it increasingly difficult to maintain his silence. He had hoped that Father Tomás would bring it up himself, and he had been particularly hopeful the first time the priest had brought out the big book. But the priest had so far not mentioned it. 'Squani badly wanted to learn to read the Spanish language.

In addition to his studies, 'Squani was assigned certain duties by the *padre,* most of which had to do with taking care of the priest's personal needs. 'Squani's command of the Spanish language had improved to the point where he could carry on a normal conversation with almost any

Spanish speaker. He had been given Spanish clothing, and his hair was growing out nicely. He thought that he was making good progress on his way to becoming a real Spaniard.

One morning after attending to the priest's early morning needs, 'Squani was all set to hear more tales from the Bible when Father Tomás settled down behind his writing table.

"Fortunato," he said, "I have a good deal of correspondence to take care of today. Spend the day in contemplation of what you've learned so far, and we'll continue tomorrow. Go now, and leave me alone."

For the first time since his arrival on the island, 'Squani found himself with a free day. He left the hut in which he lived and worked with the priest and stood looking around the unfinished outpost. He noticed some of the soldiers giving him scornful looks as they passed him by, but he was used to that.

He walked away from the hut that was his home and began to stroll around the outpost. He walked past some women, *Indios,* of course, who were busy grinding corn. He saw some Spanish soldiers engaged in what he assumed to be some kind of gambling game.

He kept walking, and soon he was watching the *Indio* slaves at work on a new hut. He stood and watched. Some were cutting down trees. Others were busy trimming the trees that had already been cut. Still others were stacking logs to make walls for the new building. Now and then a Spaniard would shout something at the *Indios* for not working fast enough or not doing something correctly.

One of the Spaniards who watched carefully and occasionally shouted was a heavyset man with dark hair and beard. His skin and his hair appeared to be oily, and the expression on his face was a perpetual scowl. He carried in his right hand a coiled length of lash.

Two of the workers finished notching the ends of a trimmed log and moved over to start on another. Two more workers moved to pick up the freshly notched log. One of them seemed to 'Squani to be particularly weak. He moved slowly, and he lifted his end of the log with obvious difficulty and pain. The man with the lash moved toward him.

"You there," he said. "Stop fooling around. Get a move on."

The *Indio* looked at the Spaniard with fear in his eyes. 'Squani thought, the man probably doesn't even understand what's being said to him.

"Get that log over there," said the Spaniard, gesturing toward the wall with his lash. The *Indio* looked confused, and the Spaniard uncoiled his lash and swung it hard, cutting across the back of the defenseless slave. The man screamed in pain and dropped the end of the log, falling to his knees. The Spaniard lashed again and again. The *Indio* lay almost motionless on his face. The Spaniard quit swinging his lash.

"Get up," he shouted.

The man tried to raise himself to his feet, but he was too weak. He fell again on his face. The Spaniard looked over his shoulder and called out to two more Spaniards behind him.

"Drag him away and give him to the dogs," he said. The two men rushed forward, each grabbing the poor fallen man by an arm, and they dragged him away, somewhere out of sight. 'Squani watched, horrified. This was the sort of cruelty that Deadwood Lighter had described in his tale of the De Soto expedition, but hearing it told was one thing. Watching it happen was something else again.

He was standing there, still stunned, when the Spaniard with the lash stepped toward him and raised his right arm to point toward 'Squani with the lash.

"You there," he said.

"Me, *señor?*" said 'Squani.

"Of course you, you ass. Who else? Do you see anyone else over there?"

"No, *señor.*"

"Get over here and take that man's place."

'Squani hesitated.

"Hurry it up," said the Spaniard, and he raised his right arm as if to lash out at 'Squani. A voice from behind stopped him.

"I wouldn't do that if I were you, Alonso."

The man with the whip, Alonso, turned his head to look, and so did 'Squani. There stood Capitán Marcos Zavala. He had a smile on his face.

"That is Fortunato," said Zavala. "Our *padre*'s pet. If you harm him, I'll never hear the end of it from that nagging priest, and if he comes nagging at me because of you, Alonso Velarde, I may throw you to the dogs."

"Pardon me, *Capitán,*" said Velarde, "I didn't know. I thought he was just another *Indio.*"

"Make do with what you have, Alonso," said Zavala.

"*Sí, Capitán.*"

Velarde turned back to the working *Indios* with renewed fervor, cracking his whip and shouting. Capitán Zavala strolled over toward 'Squani.

"Fortunato," he said, "you are indeed fortunate that I came along when I did."

"*Sí, Capitán,*" said 'Squani. "I am grateful to you."

"Yes, I'm sure you are. How is it that our Father Tomás has set you loose today?"

"He told me that he had some correspondence to take care of today," said 'Squani. "He said that I should spend the day reflecting on what I've learned."

"And what have you learned from Father Tomás?"

"He's been telling me the tales from the Bible," said 'Squani. "I know about Adam and Eve in the Garden of Eden, and the serpent, and Cain and Abel and the Land of Nod and—"

"Yes, yes," said Zavala. "And is that what you came all this way to learn?"

"I came to learn how to be a real Spaniard."

Zavala sighed a long and heavy sigh.

"Ah, Fortunato," he said, "you poor fool. You'd have been better off if I'd let you keep your sword and taught you to be a soldier, but I sacrificed you to the priest for the sake of my peace of mind."

TEN

'SQUANI did not sleep well that night. His head was full of confusion and horror. The image of Alonso Velarde lashing the helpless *Indio* kept replaying in his mind. And even worse was the image that his imagination kept conjuring up against his will, the image of the wretched, nearly dead man being thrown to the vicious big

Spanish dogs.

'Squani had heard the order given, had seen the man dragged away, and later he had heard the screams of the man and the baying and growling of the dogs. 'Squani had seen some violence in his lifetime. Occasionally a raiding party from one of the traditional enemies of the Real People would venture into their country for an attack, and when that happened, some of the Real People would retaliate. 'Squani had seen violence, but nothing like the calculated, calm cruelty of the Spaniards.

And he recalled the tales of terror told by Deadwood Lighter of the brutality of the Spaniards who followed De Soto.

But he also recalled the miserable sense of isolation he had lived with all his years in Kituwah, and the fact that he was not truly a Real Person. No clan had ever wanted him. His mother was a Timucua, and his father a nameless faceless Spanish soldier who had forced himself on her.

And he kept reminding himself that it was because of the way in which the people of Kituwah had shunned him throughout his life that he decided to become a Spaniard. But now he discovered that there were two kinds of Spaniards. There were the soldiers like De Soto and Velarde and Zavala, and there were priests like Father Tomás.

Father Tomás did not inflict cruelties on people. He did not even carry weapons. He read his big book, and he prayed. He was a teacher and a teller of tales. And the tales were another part of the confusion in the mind of 'Squani.

In many ways they were like the tales he had grown up with. They seemed to tell the story of the origin of a tribe of people called Jews. They illustrated proper behavior, and they showed what could happen to people who behaved wrongly. Yet the priest insisted that they were the only true tales, and that they were for all people. 'Squani was willing to accept the stories for himself, for he wanted to become a Spaniard. But he could not quite imagine that the stories really had any meaning or application for the Real People.

His choice had seemed simple enough when he had left Kituwah. He had been raised as a Real Person but without the status of a Real Person. He was half Spanish. He had decided to leave the Real People and become a Spaniard. But now, in the midst of the Spaniards, the choice did not seem so simple. He tried to tell himself that it might be more difficult to become a Spaniard than he had thought but that if he remained determined, he could still accomplish his purpose. At last he slept, but he slept fitfully.

He came awake when he felt someone shaking him by the shoulder. His eyes opened slowly and took in the bleary image of the priest standing over him.

"Wake up. Wake up, my son. You've overslept."

'Squani sat up, rubbing his eyes.

"I'm sorry, Father," he said.

"You had a bad night. I heard you tossing in your sleep, groaning, even talking."

"What did I say?"

"Nothing I could understand. But I think I know the source of your trouble. I heard about your adventure yesterday. It was a horrible thing for you to witness. I do my best with these rough soldiers, but they don't respond well to Christian preaching. Not until they're about to die. Then they worry about their souls. Get up now and dress. We have work to do."

They had a modest meal, and then the priest sat behind his table with 'Squani across from him. The big book was on the table in front of the priest. It was the usual setting for their lessons. The priest looked across the table at 'Squani and then back down at his book. He opened the book.

"My poor Fortunato," he said. "It's time, I think, that you learned of our Saviour."

"The one whose coming was prophesied, Father?"

"Yes. You see, Fortunato, the Bible is divided into two parts. They're called the Old Testament and the New Testament. Your lessons so far have been from the Old Testament. The New Testament tells of the coming of the Saviour."

"You mean, he's been here already?"

"Yes, my son. He came to earth to save all men."

"All men?"

"Yes. All men."

"But he didn't save the *Indio* yesterday from the dogs."

"All men will be saved, Fortunato," said the priest, "if they will but believe in the Saviour. That unfortunate soul yesterday never had a chance. Zavala refuses to allow me the time to preach to the *Indios* he has enslaved. One of my hopes for you is that with your knowledge of languages, when you have once accepted the Saviour, you will help me in my task of saving the souls of your unfortunate heathen brethren."

"All I have to do to be saved is to believe?"

"Yes. That's all. But let me start at the beginning. You see, there came a day when God looked down on the world, and he saw that it was not good. People had turned away from him and had taken up evil ways. They worshiped false gods and sought after the pleasures of the flesh.

"And God decided that it was time for him to send his Son among men to teach them the right way and to offer them a way to save their souls. And so Jesus, the Son of God, was born to the Virgin Mary.

"When he grew to manhood, he preached to the people, and he offered them a new life. He taught that God is love. He taught that we should love our enemies as ourselves. He brought a new message of love.

"But there were those who did not believe, and they did not want the new message to be heard, and so they killed our Saviour. They nailed him to the cross."

Father Tomás gestured toward the wall where a small cross was hanging. There was the figure of a man nailed to the cross. 'Squani had seen it before and had wondered about it, but now he looked at it with new interest. So that was the Saviour, and he was nailed there to die. It must have been a horrible death, he thought.

"That is Jesus?" he said.

"Yes. You see, Fortunato, he gave his life to pay for all our sins. He gave his life that we all might be saved. God the Father gave his Son that we all might have everlasting life. And all we have to do is just believe in him."

'Squani could understand sacrifice, yet there were parts of the story which puzzled him. If Jesus came to save all men, why did those men kill him? Who were they? He hesitated to ask the priest, for sometimes questions seemed to anger him. Yet he seemed remarkably gentle this day.

"Father Tomás," said 'Squani, "who were the men who killed the Saviour?"

"They were unbelievers," said the *padre*. "And their souls will roast eternally in the flames of hell, as will the souls of all those who fail to profess belief in our Lord Jesus Christ and be baptized and become Christians."

"And where will the souls of the Christians go?"

"They will go to heaven and dwell forever in the glorious presence of God."

'Squani thought for a long moment before daring to ask his next question.

"Father," he said, "is Alonso Velarde a Christian?"

"Yes," said the *padre,* "he is. Spain is a Christian land."

"Then will he go to heaven?"

"Yes, my son, he will, but first his soul will have much to atone for. You see, there is a place between heaven and hell which we call purgatory. A Christian like Alonso, who has professed his faith and then sinned again, will go to purgatory for a time to burn and purge away his sins before his soul will be admitted to the presence of God.

"Fortunato, the time is drawing near when you will have to profess your belief, when I will baptize you. But first you must be sure. You must believe. You can have no questions about your belief. You must be ready to give yourself over entirely to God the Father through love of his son Jesus Christ.

"Go now, and think about all that I have said. It's a great deal for you to take in all at once, I know. When at last you feel comfortable with what you've heard this morning, we'll talk some more. Go now."

"Where shall I go, Father?" asked 'Squani.

"Go where you will. Go where you can think about Jesus and God and be undisturbed. Go with God."

'Squani left the hovel that he called home and wandered, not through the outpost, but away from it. He wandered through the woods and listened to its sounds, and he wandered out of the woods again to the clearing the Spaniards had created around its edge. He sat down on the sandy soil and stared out at the vast ocean. It seemed that it did not go anywhere, that it was the end of the world, and yet the Spaniards had come from somewhere across that ocean in big boats. He had heard that, and he had no reason to disbelieve it. After all, they had to come from somewhere. He listened to the soothing sounds of the waves lapping the shoreline, and soon he fell asleep.

Bloody Hands and Bull Head, two of the Wolves sent out by Trotting Wolf, came upon an abandoned town in the country of the Catawbas. They were on a hillside looking down. They could tell that there was no one in the town, and even from that distance, they could tell that the place had been neglected for some time. Several houses were caved in, and one section of the wall which encircled the town had fallen over. There was no evidence that anyone had ever attempted to repair it.

"Should we go down and look more closely?" asked Bloody Hands.

"We might be able to learn something more if we go inside the town," said Bull Head.

"Then let's go."

Bloody Hands led the way down the hillside at a trot. When they reached the town walls, instead of going through the passageway, they crossed through the opening where the wall had collapsed.

"Do you think that it just fell down from age and neglect?" asked Bloody Hands.

"It's hard to tell," said Bull Head, "but I don't think so. I think it was knocked down from outside. Let's look some more."

They went inside the first house they came to, but there was nothing there.

"If the people who lived here moved away because of the land," said Bloody Hands, "they would have taken all their belongings."

"Yes," said Bull Head, "but if some enemy killed them or drove them off, the victor might have carried away all of the things the inhabitants left behind."

They left that house and looked into two more with the same results. Then Bloody Hands gestured toward the large townhouse.

"Let's look in there," he said.

They stepped inside the townhouse and stood for a moment to allow their eyes to adjust to the darkness in there. Bull Head touched Bloody Hands on the shoulder and pointed across the room.

"Look," he said.

"Is it a dead man?" asked Bloody Hands.

"Let's go closer."

They walked slowly, and as they drew closer they could see that they were indeed looking at a body. It was mostly bones, but its clothing was strange to them.

"What do you think?" asked Bull Head.

"I think that it must be a white man," said Bloody Hands. "The clothing is very strange."

He walked closer and knelt beside the body. Then, slipping his war club out of his belt, he reached out and tapped the breastplate. Eyes wide, he looked up at his partner.

"It sounds like a very hard metal," said Bull Head.

"Yes," said Bloody Hands. "That's what they say the *Ani-'squani* wear. This must be one of them."

"Then there must have been a fight here between the *Ani-Asquani* and the Catawba People," said Bull Head.

"There are no Catawba People here. The *Ani-'squani* must have driven them off."

Bloody Hands stood up and backed away from the body to stand again beside Bull Head.

"But if the *Ani-'squani* won the fight," said Bull Head, "why did they leave this one behind?"

"I don't know. From what we've heard, they're a very strange people. They do many things that we can't explain."

"Have we seen enough here?" said Bull Head.

"Yes," said Bloody Hands. "I think so. We know that the *Ani-'squani* have been here. We know they fought the Catawbas. There's nothing more we need to know about this place. Let's go."

They left the town the same way they had gone in, and they hurried across the road and up onto the hillside again. They stopped for a moment and looked back over the town.

"Where will we go now?" asked Bull Head.

"We still haven't found out where the *Ani-'squani* are

now. We have to keep looking."

"So where will we look?"

Bloody Hands looked around. He took a deep breath and exhaled in a loud sigh. Then he raised his arm and pointed.

"To the east," he said. "We'll look to the east."

ELEVEN

'SQUANI left the sandy beach and walked into the woods, making his way casually to the freshwater spring that ran through the middle of the island. He had intended to be alone for more contemplation, but there before him, kneeling at the water's edge, washing some Spaniard's shirt, was a young woman, an *Indio*. He had seen her before, grinding corn, but he had not paid her any attention. His mind had been occupied with other things.

But seeing her like this, away from the compound, away from the Spaniards, he noticed that she was not only young, but very attractive. He walked toward her, and his foot slipped on a rock. The noise startled her.

"It's all right," said 'Squani, speaking Spanish. "I'm not going to hurt you."

She answered him in a language he did not understand.

"You don't speak Spanish?" he asked, still using that language. She just stared at him with fear on her face. He decided to try the trade language. "Do you understand this tongue?" he said.

"Yes," she said.

"Don't be afraid of me," he said. "I'm not going to hurt you. What's your name?"

"The white men call me Osa," she said. "I don't know what that means, but I've learned to answer to that name."

'Squani smiled.

"It means a she-bear," he said. "Osa."

"She-bear. Why do they call me that?"

'Squani shrugged.

"I don't know. How could I know? You certainly don't look like a bear. I haven't seen much of you, but you don't seem to act like a bear."

"The first time one of them—" She paused and thought for a moment. "I scratched him."

"Oh," said 'Squani. "That's probably the reason. Where are you from, Osa?"

"I come from a village not far from here. They burned it. It was a Catawba town. Most of the men and women working here came from that town and two others. All three towns were Catawba towns."

'Squani wondered if the three towns Osa mentioned were the ones he had seen. He wondered if the Catawbas had killed the Spaniard he had found in one of those towns. Then he thought about his Spanish sword, and he wished that Capitán Zavala had not taken it away from him. Things on the Spanish island were not going for him exactly the way he had imagined them. But then, he told himself, things would change. When he had learned all he needed to know in order to be a real Spaniard, things would change.

Osa rinsed the shirt in the stream and wrung it out. Then she stood up. She looked, not at 'Squani, but at the ground between them.

"I have to get back," she said.

"Do you have to go so soon?" asked 'Squani.

"Yes. They'll be looking for me."

"Maybe we'll get another chance to talk," said 'Squani.

"Maybe," she said, and she turned and started down a path which ran through the woods and would lead her back to the compound. 'Squani watched her until she was out of sight. He wanted to see more of her. He told himself that he would.

Bloody Hands and Bull Head had reached the broad expanse of prairie between the mountains of the Real People and the seacoast to the east. They had agreed that the discovery of one Spaniard's body was not enough for them to go back home and report. Trotting Wolf would want to know for sure if there was Spanish activity in the area. He would want to know just where the Spaniards were, how many of them there were and, if possible, the nature of their activity. So they continued east.

Bull Head stretched out a hand and placed it against the chest of his companion. The two men stopped walking, and Bull Head gestured ahead and to his left. Bloody Hands looked in that direction, and he saw there a party of six men. They did not appear to be white men.

"Catawbas, do you think?" he asked.

"We're in their country," said Bull Head.

"Yes, but their towns are all abandoned."

Bull Head shrugged.

"Should we avoid them," he asked, "or not?"

"If we meet them," said Bloody Hands, "they might want to fight. There are six of them and two of us."

"They might know something about the *Ani-Asquani,*"

said Bull Head. "If we avoid them, we'll never know."

"So what should we do?"

"The worst of our two choices is that we may have to fight," said Bull Head. "Can you fight three Catawbas?"

"Ha," said Bloody Hands. "I could fight all six."

"Then let's go meet them and find out whether they'd rather talk or fight," said Bull Head. "Come on."

They walked directly toward the six men, and they watched as the men caught sight of them. They saw one of the men point toward them. Then the men lined themselves up as if bracing for an attack. The line started moving slowly forward. About a stone's throw apart, both sides stopped. They looked each other over thoroughly.

"They're Catawbas," said Bull Head.

"Yes," said Bloody Hands.

They could see that the Catawbas were talking among themselves. Then one of the Catawbas broke the silence with a shout.

"*Osiyo,*" he said. "You're Chalakees, aren't you? You see, I can speak your language."

"*'Siyo,*" said Bull Head. "Yes, we are Real People. And you speak our language well. You're Catawba People?"

"Yes. You're in our country."

"We know that," said Bull Head, "but we didn't come to fight with you."

"Then why?" said the Catawba spokesman.

"May we come closer and sit and talk?"

The Catawba spokesman said something to his companions in a low voice. Two of them shrugged. Another answered with low words. The spokesman looked back toward Bull Head and Bloody Hands.

"We have a camp back this way," he said. "Follow us there."

The camp was down by the river, and the Catawbas had fresh venison roasting there. They shared their meal with the two Real People. When all had finished eating, the Catawba spokesman, who had identified himself as Big Male Deer, spoke again.

"If you did not come into our country to fight with us," he said, "then why have you come?"

"Our people are worried about the white men who have come into this land," said Bull Head. "Our people, the Wolf People of the Real People, have closed off our country to outsiders. But that's not enough, we think. We think that we need to know where these people are and what they're doing. Some of us have gone out as scouts. We're looking for the white men."

Big Male Deer slowly nodded his head. The story made sense to him.

"I know this is your country," said Bloody Hands, "but all of your towns we've seen are abandoned. Where do you live?"

"That last town you saw," said Big Male Deer, "was our home. Now we live nowhere. Some of us roam this land looking for stray white men to kill. Sometimes they go out in small numbers."

"Where do they go out from?" asked Bull Head.

Big Male Deer pointed east.

"If you go to the edge of the land, to the big water there, you'll find an island out in the water. You can walk to it when the water's low. They're building themselves a town there. There are maybe two hundred of them. They have maybe that many of our people working there as slaves. Now and then some few of them ride out on their big dogs to look around, but mostly they're staying on the island."

"When the others came," said Bull Head, "they rode all through this land. All of them. In great numbers. They rode through towns and wiped them out. They took large numbers of slaves. They killed many people. They kept looking for the yellow metal. But you say these are just sitting on an island?"

"We, too, thought it strange," said Big Male Deer. "We've finally decided that these, unlike the others, are planning to stay. They're building houses there."

Bull Head looked at Bloody Hands.

"I think we need to go home with this news," he said.

"Yes," said Bloody Hands. "Trotting Wolf and the others will want to hear about the behavior of these men."

"Tell me, my friend," Bull Head said to Big Male Deer, "if the Real People should decide to bring many warriors through your land in order to attack the island of white men, how would your people feel about that?"

Big Male Deer spoke in his own language to his companions, and then he waited for an answer from each of them before responding to Bull Head's question.

"You know, of course," he said, "that I can only speak for myself and for my friends here, but we think that our people would welcome such a sight and even join in with you for such a purpose."

Bloody Hands cocked his head to one side for a moment as if deep in thought.

"Big Male Deer," he said, "would you and your friends return with us to our country?"

"Your country is closed to outsiders," said Big Male Deer.

"Not if you enter it in our company," said Bull Head. "I think my friend's idea is good. You can tell our people what you've told us. They can hear it directly from you."

Big Male Deer again spoke to his companions and listened to their responses. Then he stood up.

"Yes," he said. "We'll go with you, and we'll tell your people what we know about these white men."

Jacques Tournier stopped and stood in the middle of the road. Little Black Bear was already across. The others in the party were behind Tournier.

"Little Black Bear," Tournier called.

The guide stopped and turned around to face the Frenchman.

"This is the big road that goes all the way to the coast?" asked Tournier.

"Yes," said Little Black Bear.

"This is not the same place we crossed before?"

"No. When we went north, we crossed this road farther east, but it's the same road." He pointed south toward a low mountain range which ran roughly parallel to the road. "We'll cross that," he said, "and then we'll turn southeast. In another day, we'll pick up canoes and go the rest of the way to Valley Town."

"Bon," said Tournier. "And west of us here is what?"

"West of here not far is the land of the Chalaques," said Little Black Bear.

"Ah. I wish that we had been able to make contact with these Chalaques," said Tournier.

"You've made friends with the Shawnees," said the Catawba scout. "Perhaps the Chalaques will come later. Perhaps through the Shawnees."

"Or through your own people, *mon ami?*"

"My people and the Chalaques have not always gotten along well with each other," said the scout. "It might be better through the Shawnees."

"Ah, well, Rome was not built in a day."

Little Black Bear gave the Frenchman a puzzled look.

"Rome?" he asked.

"Oh, it's just a saying we have," said Tournier. "It means that things that are worthwhile sometimes take time. We'll go on back to your town, and we'll watch for our chance to meet the Chalaques. Sooner or later, we'll meet. We must."

When Bull Head and Bloody Hands and their six Catawba companions were at last getting close to the country of the Real People, they found the tracks of the white men.

"Look," said Bull Head.

"Are these white man's tracks?" asked Bloody Hands. "I've never seen tracks like these."

Big Male Deer bent to look at the tracks more closely.

"They must be white man's tracks," he said, "but they're not like the ones I've seen before. They're a little bit different. And there's another thing about these tracks."

"What's that?" asked Bull Head.

"These men, the white men and the other one, a Catawba, I think, are all walking. There are no marks made by the big dogs."

"They headed for the mountains there," said Bloody Hands.

"Should we follow them?" asked Big Male Deer.

"They're not going into our country," said Bloody Hands. "I think we should hurry into Kituwah with all of this news. There with the others we'll decide what to do."

TWELVE

Z AVALA sat across the table from Father Tomás. He sat in the chair that 'Squani used when he was getting his lessons. Zavala had come to see the priest for a purpose. He had some plans that involved the priest's pupil, and he wanted to accomplish his purpose, if possible, without getting into a quarrel with the priest. He had talked for a few minutes about nothing in particular, and he could see that Father Tomás was getting both impatient and suspicious of his motives. He decided to get to the point.

"Padre," he said, "I don't want to anger you, believe me. That's the last thing I want. I don't want to interfere in your priestly duties with young Fortunato, but I do want to suggest that if the lad is to really become civilized, he will have to know more than his catechism. So why don't you tell me when would be a good time for me to take him out for some training without disrupting your schedule?"

Father Tomás was surprised by this request from Zavala. He was even a bit irritated by it. He really wanted to keep the young *Indio* to himself. At the same time, he did not want to alienate Zavala. There were other things he would want from the *capitán* later on. Soon he would start nagging Zavala to build a church. If I give in on this, thought Father Tomás, perhaps he will give in the next time. Tit for tat.

"Just what is it, *Capitán*," asked the priest, "that you

wish to teach Fortunato?"

"How to handle a horse, to begin with," said Zavala. "He should know how to ride, don't you think?"

"And perhaps how to fight? You want to make a soldier. I want to make a scholar."

"You want to make a priestling," said Zavala, raising his voice. He checked himself. He couldn't afford to show his anger. "But I won't interfere. I've told you that. Let's just take one thing at a time. How about the riding?"

The priest stroked his chin and thought for a moment. He imagined a church and a congregation. It was a small price to pay, some riding lessons.

"Well," he said, "I don't suppose that would hurt anything, and it might be useful one of these days. All right. Between lunch and supper, tomorrow afternoon. You may have him then."

"And perhaps other afternoons?" said Zavala.

"Let's just take them one at a time," said the priest. "Perhaps."

"*Gracias, padre.* Tomorrow afternoon then," said Zavala, and he took his leave, feeling that he had accomplished half his purpose. He would pursue the other half later. There was still time.

Trotting Wolf listened carefully to the information brought into Kituwah by Bloody Hands, Bull Head and their six Catawba companions. They reported a number of abandoned towns in Catawba country due to Spanish activity, and they reported an ongoing attempt by Spaniards to establish a permanent presence on an island just off the coast, also in Catawba country. They also reported strange footprints just outside of the country of the Real People crossing the main east-west road, footprints going from north to south. They appeared to be, according to the scouts, the tracks of white men led by one Catawba man, but the Catawbas weren't sure at all that they were the tracks of Spaniards.

Trotting Wolf put this information together with that he had already heard from Breath about the six white men visiting the Shawnees. The tracks that Bloody Hands and the others reported must have been made by those six. They must have been on their way back to the Valley Town of the Catawbas. He wanted to know more about these new white men.

In the meantime, he had to make some kind of decision, and it was the kind of decision he could not make alone. It was much too important. He went to the home of his sister, Sadayi. She was not the oldest woman in the Wolf Clan, but she was very influential, and she would talk to the other women about anything of such importance and such magnitude as this current problem. He needed her advice.

And so Trotting Wolf told his sister about the reports: the Spanish outpost and the Spanish activity in the country of *Ani-Tagwa,* the Catawba People, the other white people in the area who stayed with the Catawbas and who seemed to be of a different tribe than the *Ani-Asquani,* in fact, were thought by the Catawbas to be their enemies. He finished telling about the reports, and he sat as if deep in thought for a long, silent moment.

"I think that we need to do something," he said at last. "I think that we should not just sit here guarding our borders, waiting for something to come our way. Things are hapɔening out there around us that may have an effect on us ɔne of these days. They could turn out to be big things. The Catawbas, I think, waited too long."

It was Sadayi's turn, and she, too, took a long moment to think.

"You were right to come here," she said. "I'll have to talk with the other women. Not just the Wolf Clan women, but women from all seven clans. Come back in four days. We'll talk again then."

It was the answer he'd expected to get. Still, Trotting Wolf left his sister's house feeling a little like he was being restrained. He was anxious to do something. It would be a long four days.

Father Tomás told 'Squani more stories about Jesus. He went back to the beginning and told them all in more detail. 'Squani heard about the prophecies again, and he heard about the wise men from the east and about the wicked King Herod. He heard about Jesus' youth, his baptism and his temptation. Then he heard about his preaching and about the miracles he performed. But 'Squani was particularly interested in the story of the temptation of Christ Jesus by the Devil.

"Father," asked 'Squani, "who is the Devil?"

"*El Diablo,* who is also called Satan, is a fallen angel," said Father Tomás. "In heaven, he was especially loved by God, but he was proud, and he thought that he could rule heaven and earth in the place of God. And so he rebelled against God, and for that, God cast him out of heaven and banished him forever to hell.

"The Devil hates God, and therefore he works his evil on

earth. He tries to tempt men to do evil instead of good. He tries to steal our souls away from God the Father by tempting us to do evil. When you think about doing wrong that is the Devil at work in you. And when that happens you must fight against the Devil and always do right. Ther will the Devil run screaming back to the flames of hell."

"Father," asked 'Squani, "where is hell?"

"It is deep in the bowels of this earth," said the priest.

'Squani wondered if hell was the same as the world the Real People told tales of, the world beneath this one where the seasons are the opposite of the ones on earth, where day and night are opposite, where the great monsters of the old tales are said to live. The Devil was frightening, but he was no more dreadful to think about than was the *uk'ten'*.

In the afternoons after his lessons with the priest and after his lunch, 'Squani went out with Capitán Zavala to ride. Zavala taught him to catch a horse and to saddle and bridle it. He taught him how to mount and how to ride, how to guide the animal with the reins, how to make it walk or trot or run. 'Squani liked the sessions with the *caballos,* and he took to riding almost naturally. He liked the animals, and he liked to ride. He thought about Deadwood Lighter, who had also learned to ride. He recalled how much he had admired and envied the old man, and he was proud that he was learning all of the things that Deadwood Lighter had learned.

They had just put away the horses. It was time for 'Squani to return to the priest's hut for supper.

"Fortunato," said Zavala, "I'm going to ask the *padre* to let you go with me for a few days."

'Squani turned to look Zavala in the face. It was getting to be much easier for him to do that.

"Where will we go, *Capitán?*" he asked.

"I'm taking some of the soldiers to the mainland on an excursion," said Zavala. "Just to look around. I want you to ride along with us."

'Squani was taken by surprise, and he found the prospect of riding out on horseback with the Spanish soldiers to be very exciting.

"I want to go," he said, "but what will Father Tomás say?"

"If you tell him you want to go," said Zavala, "he may relent. If he refuses his permission, I can take you with me anyway. He's not in charge here. I am. But if I can keep from getting him angry, that will be the best way."

"I'll ask him if I can go," said 'Squani.

"Bueno," said Zavala.

"Capitán?"

"Sí?"

"May I carry my sword?"

Zavala laughed out loud, and 'Squani's face burned with embarrassment.

"We'll see, Spaniard," said Zavala. "We'll see."

On his way back to the priest's hut, 'Squani saw Osa. She was alone, just walking back into the compound from the woods. She passed by a building that was still under construction. 'Squani hurried to meet her, but he tried to act as if he had come upon her by accident.

"Hello," he said, using the trade language.

"Hello," she answered, looking at the ground. She

started to move on.

"Wait," said 'Squani. "Do you remember me? They call me Fortunato. I remember you. You're Osa, the she-bear.'

"Yes," she said. "I remember."

"I've been wanting to see you again."

"You have?" she said. "Why?"

"I don't know. I like talking to you."

"Do you want me to come to your bed tonight?" she asked.

'Squani was startled by the abruptness of that question, and his face betrayed his emotion. Osa looked at him with curiosity.

"What's wrong?" she asked. "That's what the others always want with me. That's all they want. Aren't you one of them?"

For the first time since his arrival at the Spanish compound, 'Squani was not so anxious to identify himself as a Spaniard.

"My father was one of them," he said. "My mother is a Timucua woman."

"You speak their language," said Osa.

"Yes. I've learned it."

"You're not a slave here."

"That's because of my father, I guess. I'm learning about the way they live."

"I have to go," said Osa. "The one with red hair will be looking for me."

'Squani watched her as she walked away, and then he saw the man she had mentioned. A big Spaniard with red hair and beard, he took Osa by her arm and pulled her into a hut. 'Squani was suddenly overcome with rage, but it was a helpless rage. There was nothing he could do but try to swallow it.

He went to bed that night with images of naked women being covered by brutal, ugly, dirty Spaniards, and the women he saw were Osa and his own mother. And sometimes the brutal Spaniard in the image was 'Squani himself.

Sadayi met with the other women of her clan, and then she sent for her brother Trotting Wolf. He tried not to appear too anxious, but he was. For four days he had been waiting for her. He had passed the time in visiting with the Catawbas who were in Kituwah as guests, and he talked with other Wolves when they came in from their positions guarding the passes or from their scouting trips. Not one had come in with any new information, though.

When Trotting Wolf walked up to his sister's house, she was there with three other women from the clan. She did all the talking.

"We think that you should take some men with you, brother," she said, "and go with the *Ani-Tagwa* back to their town, their Valley Town. We think that you should meet with these new white men and find out what they're like. If they're really enemies of these others, these *Ani-Asquani,* then you could join with the new white men and the Catawbas. Together you should be able to wipe out these *Ani-'squani,* or at least, run them out of this land. That's what we think. We've all talked it over."

It was just what Trotting Wolf had wanted to hear. Of course, it would take time. He would have to talk to the Catawbas again and find out what their feelings were. He was pretty sure that he knew, but they hadn't really talked about anything like attacking the island. He'd have to talk to them more specifically.

Then a general council of all the people in town would have to be called before they could actually set out, and even if everyone finally agreed that the right thing to do was to make war on the Spaniards, there would be ritual preparations to go through. It would all take time, and Trotting Wolf was anxious to get started.

THIRTEEN

B Y design, he met her at the stream in the woods. It was late at night. Her company had not been demanded that night by any of the soldiers, and he had waited until the priest was asleep and snoring. Then he had sneaked out of the hut and made his way through the woods to meet her. She had been much on his mind.

"I'm glad you came," he said.

"What do you want me to do?" she asked. She was not looking at him. She was looking into the stream. It made a pleasant rippling sound as it ran its course.

"Nothing but this," he said. "To see you. To talk with you. That's all."

"You're not like the others," she said. "But you weren't raised by them, were you?"

"No," he said, not quite knowing how he felt about this matter anymore. "I was raised by—*Indios*."

"And you came here on purpose? You weren't captured?"

"That's right."

"Why?"

"Because my mother was Timucua and my father a Spaniard, among the Chalakees, I had no clan. I was never really one of them. I came here because of my father."

"Do you think you can find him?" she asked.

"No. I'll never find him," he said. "I wouldn't know him if I saw him. And he doesn't even know he's my father. My mother wouldn't know him. There were too many of them. She was—"

"Like me," she said.

"Yes."

They sat for a long moment in silence. It was a solemn moment, almost sad.

"I came here because my father was Spanish," he said, "and I thought that maybe the Spaniards would accept me as one of them."

"Have they accepted you?"

"I don't know," he said. "I'm learning to speak the language better. I'm learning the stories from the big book, and now I'm learning to ride the *caballos*. I guess maybe they've accepted me."

"Then you should be happy," she said. "You have what you want."

"Yes," he said, but even he knew that he did not sound convinced.

"When you learn more," she asked, "will you be as cruel as the others?"

"No," he said. "They're not all cruel. Father Tomás is a good man. He's a priest. A man of God."

But he thought about the way Father Tomás looked when he didn't like the questions he was asked. He thought about the anger he had heard more than once in the priest's voice. He looked at her, and she shrugged.

"I don't know the priest," she said. "I know the others."

"I'm going to ride off the island with them soon," he said. "They're going out to look around, and they want me to go with them."

"Are you going to catch more slaves?" she asked.

"No."

"They always bring back slaves," she said, "unless the people fight them. Then they kill the people. But they always try to bring more slaves."

"Not this time. Capitán Zavala himself told me that we were just going out to look around."

"Two more men died today," she said. "They want more workers. But you'll see what they do when you go out with them."

"Yes," he said. "I'll see. And when we come back, I'll tell you about it. I think we'd better return now. I'm afraid that Father Tomás might wake up and miss me."

Back in his bed inside the hut, 'Squani lay awake thinking about what she had said. He thought about the slaves being worked to death. He thought about the lovely young woman being used by the soldiers at their will and against her own. Mostly he thought about one question she had asked him: "When you learn more, will you be as cruel as the others?"

He felt good mounted on the big *caballo*. Capitán Zavala was riding right beside him. The other men were behind. The horses were stamping and ready to go. It was all the men could do to hold them back. The weapons and the armor of the men were clanking behind him. It was all very exciting.

They were ready to ride out, but Capitán Zavala had not yet given the word. 'Squani struggled with his spirited mount. It was taking all of his attention to control it. He barely heard the captain speak to him.

"Fortunato."

'Squani glanced over toward the captain and saw that he was holding out toward him a sword in a scabbard on a wide leather belt.

"Take it, Fortunato," said Zavala. "Put it on. It's a better one than your old one. This one is new. It's not even yet tasted blood. Here. Take it."

'Squani reached out and took the sword. It was not easy strapping the belt around his waist while trying to control the eager *caballo,* but 'Squani at last managed it. Zavala laughed good-naturedly, then raised his right hand.

"Come on," he said. "Let's ride."

He led the way, 'Squani riding by his side. They rode through the trees to the clearing and then to the water's edge. They splashed through the shallow water across to the tip of the peninsula and then up onto dry land again. Then they rode the length of the narrow peninsula and arrived on the mainland. From there, Zavala turned north.

It was the longest ride 'Squani had yet taken, and for a good while, just the ride was enough. He felt a feeling of freedom and power that he had never known before. The speed and strength of the horse beneath him were his to command. And he was riding almost at the head of a mounted troop of Spanish soldiers.

But eventually he began to wonder where they were

going and what their purpose might be. They had crossed the main east-west road and were riding a small trail almost due north. Zavala had said that they were just going out to look around, but it didn't seem that way.

They rode straight ahead, as if with a purpose. They rode as if headed toward some specific destination. Zavala did not slow down. He did not look to his left or his right. He looked straight ahead. They stopped once to eat, and then they mounted up again and rode some more. When next they stopped, the sun was low in the western sky, and 'Squani knew that they would not be returning to the island that day.

They made their camp and ate their evening meal, and then they lay down on the ground to sleep. 'Squani's thighs ached on the insides. Early that morning, mounting up, he had thought that he was a horseman. That night, sore and tired, he wasn't so sure.

They were up and riding again early the following morning. 'Squani groaned when he climbed back into the saddle, and for a while he thought that he wouldn't be able to endure the pain. Eventually, though, he became numb to it. Zavala must have noticed.

"Fortunato," he called, a wide smile on his face, "how is your ass today?"

"What, *Capitán?*" asked 'Squani.

"Your ass. Your *nalga.* The part of you on which you sit," the captain shouted.

The soldiers to the rear who were near enough to hear began to laugh, and Zavala laughed with them. 'Squani waited for the laughter to subside before he answered Zavala.

"I'm all right," he said.

"Ah," said Zavala, "Fortunato, I believe that your father was indeed *Español,* a real hard-ass, a leather breeches. You'll be just fine, Fortunato. You'll make a real *caballero* if the god damned priest doesn't ruin you first."

They rode until the sun was directly overhead, and then they stopped again to eat. After a meal and a short rest, they mounted up and rode again. The afternoon was half done when they came to the village. 'Squani could not decide whether the people there were surprised or simply did not know that the Spaniards meant them harm. At any rate, they were at home, and they were not prepared to fight.

Seven of them came out to meet the Spaniards. They waved and called out some kind of greeting. 'Squani did not understand the language they spoke.

"Fortunato," said Zavala, "can you speak to these people?"

"If they speak the trade language I can," said 'Squani.

"Well, give it a try then."

"Do any of you speak the trade language?" asked 'Squani in a loud voice.

"Yes," said an old man. "I speak it. Welcome to our town. Come in and eat with us. We're friends."

'Squani translated for Zavala.

"Tell him we'll eat with them," said Zavala. "Tell him who I am. And ask his name, and find out what people these are."

'Squani did as Zavala ordered, and the old man answered.

"We are Waccamaw. My name is the Black Warrior. I'm

the chief of this village."

Zavala and the others dismounted, and they followed the Black Warrior into the village. Men came out to meet them. Women were busy preparing food. Children hid inside houses or peered around the corners. Dogs barked.

The Black Warrior led the way to the townhouse and inside, where everyone was seated. The food was brought in, and everyone ate his fill. 'Squani noticed the way the Spanish soldiers looked at the women who were serving them. Now and then, a Spaniard would actually put a hand on one of the women. Zavala noticed too.

"You men behave like gentlemen tonight," he said. "We're going to sleep here, and I don't want any problems during the night. Don't do anything to upset these people. Leave the women alone."

Some of the men groaned out loud, but no one argued with Zavala. 'Squani was relieved to hear Zavala's orders. He was thinking about what he would tell Osa when he next saw her. He would tell her that Zavala had actually ordered the men to be polite to these Waccamaw People. She wouldn't be able to argue with that.

They slept in the townhouse that night, and 'Squani slept soundly. He was awakened in the morning by Zavala's voice. The captain ordered everyone up and dressed. He called out to the Black Warrior for food. 'Squani noticed right away that Zavala was not as polite as he had been the night before.

After they had eaten, Zavala had 'Squani call the Black Warrior into the townhouse for talk.

"Tell him that I need twenty strong young men," said the

captain, "and ten young women."

"Need them for what, *Capitán?*" asked 'Squani.

"To go with us back to the island," said Zavala. "What else?"

'Squani spoke to the Black Warrior, but before the old man could respond, Zavala spoke again.

"Tell him that if the men and women fail to report to me here, I'll have him killed."

'Squani hesitated, more than a little horrified by the bluntness and brutality of this last statement.

"Tell him," said Zavala.

'Squani told the chief what Zavala had said.

"I'm an old man," said the Black Warrior. "I don't have much time left anyway. Tell him to kill me."

'Squani translated for Zavala. Zavala smiled and stood up, drawing his sword. He walked to the door of the town-house.

"Come here, Fortunato," he said.

'Squani walked over to stand beside the captain. Zavala looked outside. He put a hand on 'Squani's shoulder.

"You see that man out there?" he asked.

"Sí, señor."

"Tell him what I want, and tell him that if I don't get it, I'll kill the old chief."

'Squani walked outside and stepped toward the man.

"Do you speak the trade language?"

"Yes."

"My chief wants twenty young men and ten young women to return with us to our village," 'Squani said. "If they refuse, he's going to kill the Black Warrior. Talk to them. Tell them to come in and offer themselves. We'll take them and leave, and no harm will come to anyone else."

"I'll tell them," said the man, and soon twenty Waccamaw men and ten Waccamaw women came into the townhouse. The man 'Squani had spoken to outside walked up to him.

"They're ready to go," he said. "Tell him not to harm our chief."

FOURTEEN

"FÉLIX," said Zavala, and Félix Ocampo ran over to stand before his commander.

"Sí, Capitán," he said.

"Line them all up and march them outside in single file."

With only a little difficulty, Ocampo accomplished that task. The Spaniards, including 'Squani, all followed the newly acquired slaves outside.

"Now, Félix," said Zavala, "send a man to get the horses ready. And while we're waiting, tie these together. We have a long ride ahead of us. We need to get started."

Ocampo ordered one man to go for the horses and another to take charge of the binding of the slaves. 'Squani wondered why, when the men and women had come voluntarily, Zavala saw a need to bind them. He watched as the Spanish soldiers pulled the men's arms behind their backs and tied their wrists together. About half of the men had been so tied when the horses were brought around.

Then a soldier went to the first man in line. He tied a new line to the man's wrists, which were already bound, then ran the new line back to the next man. He tied the loose end of the line around the neck of the second man. Then he moved around behind the second man to repeat the process.

Eight men had their hands tied behind them, and the first three men had been linked together when the next-to-last man standing in line broke and ran. Zavala shouted.

"Félix," he roared, "keep to your job. Carranza, Ortega, Sol, mount your horses and catch that man. Bring him back alive."

The three men ran for their mounts, climbed into their saddles and raced after the fugitive. Others had drawn their swords and were standing around the remaining prisoners. 'Squani watched as if in a trance.

The binding together of the prisoners, all except the one escapee, was completed. Because of the nearness of the woods, the fugitive and his mounted pursuers were out of sight, but the shouts of the horsemen could be heard. Inside the village, everyone stood in tense silence.

At last the horsemen returned, driving before them the unhappy escapee. They shoved him toward Zavala, and he fell there, sprawling in the dirt at the captain's feet.

Zavala dropped down, placing one knee on the back of the man's neck. He took hold of the loose hanging scalp lock and pulled the man's head up, twisting it so that the man was looking toward the Black Warrior.

"I warned you what would happen," said Zavala. "Now watch."

Zavala looked at Félix Ocampo, and the eyes of the two men met. Then Zavala nodded toward the Black Warrior.

"Kill him, Félix," he said.

Ocampo walked over to stand in front of the old chief.

'Squani saw an almost imperceptible raising of one eye-brow, a subtle expression of realization on the face of the Black Warrior. Other than that, he did not move. He stood straight, his look defiant.

Ocampo drew out his sword, raised it high over his head and swung it down hard, slicing into the old man's neck and shoulder, down into his chest. The old man made hardly a noise. His head fell back, his knees buckled, and he crumpled into an insignificant-looking heap there on the ground in a widening pool of dark blood.

A shout of protest and horror came from the mouth of the one who had caused the murder, the one who had tried to escape, the one whose head was still held up by its hair, upon whose neck Zavala knelt. With his left hand, Zavala pulled back harder on the hair, stretching the neck even more. With his right he drew a knife out of a sheath at his belt, and he slit the throat of the helpless man. He casually cleaned the blade of his knife by wiping it on the man's breechclout. Then he stood up.

"Félix," he said, "we need another slave to replace this one."

"*Sí, Capitán,*" said Ocampo, but before he could do any-thing about it, before he could say more, an arrow came flying out of nowhere, and drove itself into Ocampo's ear. The man screamed and grabbed for the shaft. He dropped to his knees.

Other arrows flew. Two horses were struck. They screamed in pain and terror and stomped around. Arrows broke against Spanish breastplates. One drove itself deep into the right thigh of Marcos Zavala.

Spaniards slashed with swords at the people nearest to

hem. Two or three managed to get into their saddles, and they ran at the *Indios,* slashing with swords or jabbing with lances. One Spaniard knelt beside the door of the town-house with a crossbow, firing short shafts. His first sank into the chest of an *Indio.* The next into the back of another.

'Squani backed away from the fight. He was horrified. He pressed himself against the side of a house and watched around the corner. He did not want to fight Spaniards. He wanted to be a Spaniard. But he did not want to take part in this horrible slaughter of innocent people.

The battle was a swarm of confusion, and for a while it looked as if it could go either way. Then there was a loud explosion. The defenders of the town scattered in all directions. Spaniards chased them and shot at their backs, but soon the town was abandoned except for the conquering Spaniards and the slaves who had been tied together.

A lone dog barked defiantly, and a Spaniard skewered it with his lance. It was only then, in the quiet aftermath of the violence, that 'Squani saw the smoking pole in the Spaniard's hands, and he remembered Deadwood Lighter's description of the fire poles, the guns that spat fire and pieces of metal.

Zavala limped painfully over to the wall of the town-house, where he managed to get down into a sitting position and lean back against the wall. He called to the soldier nearest him.

"Sí, Capitán?"

"Pull this god damned arrow out of my leg," said the captain. The soldier hesitated. "Pull it out. Now."

The soldier bent over Zavala's leg and gripped the shaft

with both hands. He braced himself. Then he gave a mighty yank, tearing the arrow loose along with a bit of bloody flesh. Zavala roared out in angry pain as blood gushed from the wound.

"Stop the bleeding," said Zavala.

Another soldier came running over to where the one worked on Zavala's wounded leg.

"Capitán," he said, "two *caballos* are badly hurt."

"Put them out of their misery," said Zavala. "What about the men?"

"Three are dead," said the soldier. "Eight are wounded. One of them is Félix Ocampo. The other seven will be all right, but Félix—"

"What about him?" said Zavala.

"He has an arrow through his head. It went in through his ear hole. He's just lying there rolling his eyes and gurgling."

"Well," said Zavala, "cut his throat for him."

"Cut his throat, *Capitán?*"

"Would you do more for a horse than for a man?"

"Sí, Capitán," said the soldier. "I mean, no, *Capitán.* I'll go and cut his throat right away."

In a short while the wounded horses and Félix Ocampo had been mercifully killed. The other wounded men had been crudely patched up. Zavala had to be helped onto the back of his horse. Then he ordered the others to mount up. Four mounted men were assigned to march the slaves along behind.

"You'll catch up with us at our camp tonight," said Zavala. "And before you leave the village, burn it."

Zavala led the way. 'Squani, still stunned, rode along

beside him. Now the horses' hooves and the clanking of the soldiers' weapons and armor behind him did not seem as exciting as they had before. He looked over his shoulder once and saw black smoke rising from the village.

Suddenly, 'Squani wanted badly to be back in the hut with Father Tomás. He did not want to be a Spanish soldier. The life of the priest, studying and praying, seemed much more attractive. 'Squani was not afraid of fighting, but he found the kind of slaughter the Spaniards engaged in to be revolting. He did not know the people who had been killed back at the village, but he did not like the cold way in which the killings had been done.

They stopped to make camp early that night, perhaps to allow the ones coming from behind time to catch up. They built fires and made their beds, and they ate their evening meal. Soon the others arrived. The soldiers ate, and then they fed the slaves. 'Squani noticed that they did not feed the slaves nearly as well as they had fed themselves.

'Squani did not eat much. He was afraid that he would be sick if he tried. He tried to sleep, but he could not. He kept reliving the horrible battle at the village. The bloody images would not leave his mind. And even if he could have gotten the images to leave him alone, Zavala was tossing in his bedroll and groaning. 'Squani figured that the wound must be bothering him. As the night wore on, Zavala's tossing and groaning turned into raving. Then, incredibly, 'Squani fell into a deep sleep.

He was startled back awake by loud voices, and he saw that it was morning. Some of the soldiers were already preparing food to start the day. They were all dressed, and some were getting the horses ready. Zavala was still in his bedroll. He had a blanket pulled up close under his chin, and his eyes were rolling wildly. A soldier approached him.

"Get away," screamed Zavala. "Get away from me."

"Leave him alone," called out another soldier.

"I just thought we should try one more time."

"He's gone crazy."

"Well, what will we do with him?"

"Put him out of his misery," said one. "That's his own philosophy."

"Who's going to do it?" said another. "I'm not going to do it."

"Then leave him. Let's mount up and get out of here."

They climbed into their saddles and started to ride off. One soldier was leading Zavala's horse. He rode toward where the captain lay snarling.

"Here's your horse, *Capitán*," he said. "Do you want your horse?"

"Get away from me."

"All right," said the soldier. "Damn. Try to help someone and what do you get?"

He rode away, leading the horse. 'Squani did not feel like riding at the head of the column without Zavala there beside him, so he waited until they had all gone past, all except those escorting the slaves, and then he fell in at the end of the line. He did not look back.

Zavala watched as the last of the soldiers passed him by. His leg was black and swollen and throbbing with pain. His head was hot with fever. He wanted a drink of water.

No. Of wine. Good red wine. He wanted the pain to stop, but it was deep inside of the leg. Maybe the leg should be cut off. He wondered if he could do that to himself. His sword was sharp. Could he do it? He didn't know.

He knew that he could cut through a leg with one powerful blow of his sword, but it would be an awkward swing the way he was lying down. He might just cut into it without severing it, and only make matters worse. Or he might cut both legs. Anyway, he didn't even know where his sword was.

Crazy. He had heard someone say the word "crazy." Had it been meant to describe him? Yes. Probably. He decided that he was crazy. The horrible, pus-oozing wound, the blackness in the leg, the swelling, the throbbing pain, the fever: all were making him crazy. Then he saw the figures coming toward him. Four figures. He squinted his eyes to try to make them come into better focus. They moved slowly and deliberately. They came closer.

"Who are you?" he shouted.

The figures came closer, and he could see that they were nearly naked. *Indios?* Savages? he asked himself. Still they moved toward him.

"Who the hell are you? Answer me. God damn you. Get away. Get the hell away from me."

They came even closer, and he could see that they were indeed *Indios,* four nearly naked *Indios,* and they were armed. Each one held a stone-headed war club in his hand. He could see knives at the waists of two of them. One of them held a long, wooden, stone-tipped lance in his hand.

"Get away, you savage bastards," he shouted. He struggled to his feet, and the pain that shot through his body when he put weight on the ruined leg was almost unbearable. He screamed. He did not see as two of the men moved around behind him. One raised a war club and bashed it into his back, and Zavala felt bones snap. He staggered forward. Another swung, and Zavala felt his shoulder being crushed. He screamed again, and another war club whizzed through the air. This one shattered his jaw and knocked him sideways to the ground. He looked up just in time to see the long lance coming toward him. It touched his chest. It pressed on. He felt it enter. He felt no more.

FIFTEEN

F ATHER," said 'Squani, "I don't want to go out with the soldiers anymore. Will I have to? I want to stay with you. I want to study. I don't want to be a soldier."

"What happened out there, Fortunato?" asked the priest.

'Squani had slept the night well back in the priest's hut. He was calm, although the horror of the fight in the village remained with him, and the images were still clear in his mind.

"We rode for two days," he said. "We rode north. Then we came to a village. The people there were called Waccamaw People. I couldn't understand their language, but some of them could speak the trade language, so I was able to communicate with them. I guess that's the reason that Capitán Zavala took me along in the first place.

"The Waccamaw People were friendly and invited us into their village. They fed us and gave us a place to sleep. In the morning, Capitán Zavala had me tell them that he wanted twenty men and ten women to bring back here with him as slaves. If they refused, he said, he would kill their chief, an old man named the Black Warrior.

"Then twenty men and ten women came and offered themselves to save the Black Warrior, but when the *capitán* ordered them tied together, one of them ran."

'Squani paused. The images of horror swam in his brain.

"Go on, my son," said Father Tomás.

"They caught the man who ran, and the *capitán* ordered the Black Warrior's death. Félix Ocampo killed him with his sword. Then Capitán Zavala cut the throat of the other, the one who had run.

"When that happened, all of the men in the village began to fight. It was a terrible fight, Father. I don't know how many men were killed. But when it was over, the *Indios* had all run away, all who were still alive.

"Félix Ocampo was badly hurt, and Capitán Zavala told someone to cut his throat for him, to put him out of his misery."

Father Tomás said some words that 'Squani could not understand and made the sign of the cross.

"The captain was hurt by an arrow in his leg, but he mounted his horse and we all rode off. We camped for the night, and in the morning, the captain was like a crazy man. We left him there alone."

"Fortunato," said Father Tomás, "did you take part in this fight?"

"No, Father," said 'Squani. "Was I wrong not to fight?"

"You did right, my son. I tried to tell Zavala that his methods were wrong. He wouldn't listen to me. So now God has shown him the error of his ways. Well, God have mercy on his soul. He cannot possibly survive out there alone, hurt and mad."

"Father Tomás," a voice interrupted from outside the hut. "May I come in?"

"Who is it?" said the priest.

"It's Juan Sol."

"Come in."

Juan Sol stepped inside the hut. 'Squani recognized the man as one of those who had been along on the excursion, one of those who had taken part in the fight. Sol looked at 'Squani, then back at the priest.

"What is it, my son?" asked Father Tomás.

"Padre," said Sol, "Capitán Zavala and Félix Ocampo are both dead. There was discussion, and the leadership has fallen on my unworthy shoulders. I just came to let you know."

"I have been given to understand that Capitán Zavala was alive when last seen," said Father Tomás.

Sol ducked his head and shuffled his feet nervously.

"Well, yes," he said. "He was, but he was raving mad. He wouldn't let anyone get close to him. We tried to help him. Several of us tried. He kept yelling at us to go away and leave him alone. So at last we did. I doubt if he's alive by now, though."

"I see," said the priest.

"Well, Father, that's all I came to tell you. I won't take any more of your time."

"Juan," said Father Tomás.

Sol stopped and turned back to face the priest.

"Sí, padre?"

"Juan, since you are now in command, perhaps you can

arrange for me to have some time with the *Indios,* the workers. I need to be about my business of saving souls. Capitán Zavala never allowed me the time, you know."

"Oh, *sí, padre.* Of course. Any time you say. You just let me know, all right?"

Father Tomás smiled broadly. He stepped to Sol and put a hand on his shoulder.

"*Gracias,* Juan," he said. "*Muchas gracias,* my son. I think it is well that you are in command here, and I will write that opinion in my journal. It will be read back in España. You can be sure of that."

"Oh, thank you, Father," said Sol, and he took his leave. Father Tomás walked with a light step back to the chair behind his table. He sat down and leaned back. The smile was still on his face.

"Fortunato," he said.

"Yes, Father?"

"You told me once that you wanted to learn to read and write."

"Yes, Father."

"Come, my son," said the priest. "Take your chair. We will begin."

'Squani knew the ancient system of writing the language of the Real People, the one that had almost died with the *Ani-Kutani.* The system of the Real People had a symbol for every syllable in the language. The only exception was a symbol for the hissing sound. Thus Asquani was able to write his own name with four symbols: the ah symbol, the hissing sound symbol, the qua and the ni. With the letters of the Spaniards, he had to use seven. The system of letters at first gave 'Squani trouble. He had to use a letter that

Father Tomás called a consonant in combination with another letter called a vowel in order to accomplish what the Real People could write with only one symbol. But there were not so many symbols to learn, and soon he began to master them.

There was another problem. In writing Spanish, the same symbol could, under different circumstances, stand for different sounds. The first sound in the word *casa* was not the same as that in the word *cinco*. But there were rules for these changes, and 'Squani learned the rules.

Soon Father Tomás allowed 'Squani to sit with the big book on the table in front of him and read from it and even turn the pages for himself. And 'Squani was thrilled to read for himself the very stories that Father Tomás had told him. He had read all the way through the Book of Genesis and was ready to begin Exodus.

He was proud of himself, but careful not to show it, for Father Tomás had told him that pride was a sin. But the priest praised him for his quick progress, and so he was able to maintain an attitude of humility more easily. In general, things seemed to have gotten better since the death of Capitán Zavala. Father Tomás almost seemed to be in charge, for Juan Sol always showed great respect for the priest. Father Tomás said that Sol was a true believer, and that surely he would find his reward in heaven.

'Squani noticed, though, that Juan Sol was almost as rough with the other soldiers as Zavala had been. He growled and shouted orders, threats, obscenities and profanities. He did nothing to stem the brutality of Alonso Velarde's treatment of the slaves. But he was always meek in the presence of the priest.

And because 'Squani was the special student of the priest, the soldiers, under the command of Juan Sol, walked carefully around him.

The lot of the slaves did improve, though, with Juan Sol in charge. When they worked, they worked as hard as ever before, and they worked under the lash as before. But they did not work as much as they had before, because the priest took them away from their work in the afternoons in order to preach to them.

And for that task, 'Squani became Father Tomás's indispensable assistant. None of the *Indios* could understand Spanish, and the priest could not speak a word of their language—or languages. Most of the slaves were Catawbas, and some of them knew the jargon. 'Squani could therefore speak to them in the jargon, and the slaves who understood could translate for the others.

So Father Tomás preached in Spanish, and 'Squani translated into the trade language. Then Osa, for 'Squani had named her as one who could do the job, repeated everything in the language of the Catawbas. This became every afternoon's business.

'Squani was happy for the first time in his life. Of course, there was the unpleasant fact of the lot of the slaves, but even that had been somewhat improved. He tried to ignore their morning treatment and concentrate instead on the relief he saw in their faces in the afternoons. And many of them seemed to be really interested in the teachings of the priest.

He was Fortunato, a Spaniard, assistant to a priest. He knew the Bible, and he could read. And there was a woman, Osa. He found himself more and more interested in her.

"Father," he said one afternoon, "may I speak with you?"

"Of course, my son."

"Since we've begun the preaching in the afternoons, and the woman Osa has been translating, I think I've seen a change in her. I think that she believes."

"I hope that many, if not all, of our congregation are believing the word of God," said the priest.

"But Osa is treated like a whore," said 'Squani. "The soldiers use her that way, and it doesn't seem right to me that the one who carries your words to the *Indios* should be used that way."

Father Tomás sat for a moment as if in deep thought, and he rubbed his chin.

"Fortunato," he said, "that is an excellent observation. I'm proud of you for bringing that sad fact to my attention. I'll speak to Juan Sol at once."

The *padre* stood up to leave his hut. At the door he stopped and turned back around to face 'Squani.

"Is it about time for your baptism, my son?" he asked, a benign smile on his face.

"Yes, Father," said 'Squani. "I think that it is time. I believe the word of God. I believe in the Father and the Son and the Holy Ghost, and I believe that Jesus Christ is my Saviour. I would like very much to be baptized."

"If this woman, Osa, is also ready for baptism," said Father Tomás, "we could have a ceremony in which my first two converts are baptized. It would be wonderful. I'll be back soon. Wait for me here."

'Squani sat alone, and he felt a little guilty for the things he had said to the priest. He was not at all sure that he believed the stories from the Bible any more than he believed those told by the Real People. Perhaps he believed *all* the stories. He certainly was not convinced that the priest's tales were the only true tales.

Yet he did want to be baptized. He had not lied about that. He wanted to be baptized because he thought that was the only way he could become a real Spaniard. The Spaniards were all Christians, according to the priest, and to become a Christian one had to be baptized.

He also wanted Osa to be saved from the life she had been forced to lead by the Spanish soldiers. He liked Osa. He tried to ascribe Christian motives to his attempt to save her, but he knew that he really wanted her for himself. If Father Tomás could get her away from the soldiers and baptize them both, then 'Squani would tell the priest that he wanted to marry Osa.

He would teach her to speak Spanish, and then perhaps one day he would take her with him to Spain. He tried to imagine what Spain would be like, but he could not. Now and then he had asked Father Tomás to describe it for him, and the priest had told him that it was full of large cities with large stone buildings and streets paved with stone. But that was all, and even that was hard to imagine.

These were the thoughts that filled 'Squani's head as he sat alone, waiting impatiently for the priest to return. He hoped that he would return with Osa. And he felt just a little guilty.

SIXTEEN

T HE *padre*'s dream was a church, a church on the island where he could gather in the heathen and preach to them and save their souls for God. Now the only buildings on the island were huts, and a large arbor under which he could hold meetings. But he wanted a church.

There were more pressing needs, though. He asked Juan Sol to have another hut constructed right next to his. It would be for Osa. If she was to live the life of a Christian woman, she would need her own hut, safe from the lustful soldiers, close to the protection of the *padre*. Sol agreed, and the hut was built in a short while.

He had told 'Squani that the baptism would have to wait for the new church. He wanted to make other people as eager for the church as was he himself. And 'Squani was indeed anxious. He wanted to be a Christian, so he could be a real Spaniard.

It was late afternoon. The building was done for the day, and the afternoon preaching was concluded. The slaves had gone back to their quarters. 'Squani was in the *padre*'s hut with Osa, teaching her some Spanish words. Father Tomás walked to the hut of Juan Sol.

"May I come in?" he asked, his head already poking in the doorway.

Sol jumped up from his chair.

"Of course, *padre*," he said. "Please come in. Here. Sit in this chair. Will you have a glass of red wine with me?"

"*Sí,*" said the priest. "*Gracias.*"

Sol poured two glasses of wine and handed one to the priest. He sat on the edge of his table.

"To what do I owe the honor of this visit, *padre?*" he asked.

"Juan," said Father Tomás, "how is your work going here?"

"Well, I think it's going all right. Our orders were to establish a permanent outpost on this island. We have the buildings all done now. Of course, there are always improvements that can be made."

"A church," said Father Tomás.

"Excuse me? You said, a church?"

"Yes, my son. A church. You have the workers. What is a Christian outpost without a church? Why was I sent along with you if not to establish a church here in this wilderness? We are all engaged in God's work, Juan. Such an accomplishment will go greatly in your favor when the time comes for your soul to be judged by God."

"*Sí, padre,*" said Sol. "A church. We should build a church here. A church that all of Spain will hear about and be proud of. A fine church."

"I have plans," said the priest. "How soon can we get started?"

"Right away, Father. Tomorrow. Why should we delay?"

"Why indeed?" said the *padre*. "After all, it is God's work we're doing here."

"Yes," said Sol. "God's work."

Trotting Wolf left Kituwah with fifty Real People behind him, all tried warriors. Big Male Deer and the other five Catawbas accompanied them. Enough men of the Wolf

Clan had been left behind to guard the passes. Everything would be all right at home until the warriors returned.

Trotting Wolf had several things in mind. First and most important was driving the Spaniards out of the country. It seemed almost certain that if the Spaniards were allowed to maintain a permanent outpost on the edge of the Catawba country, it would be only a matter of time before they found their way into the country of the Real People. It made more sense to drive them out early.

In addition, this expedition would give Trotting Wolf an opportunity to meet the new white men, the Frenchmen, and find out what they were like. According to the Catawbas, they were not bad men like the Spaniards. They might turn out to be good allies. And they were looking for new trading partners. Perhaps the Real People could benefit from that. It was a chance to look them over without letting them into the country of the Real People.

Trotting Wolf and Big Male Deer led the force, and along the way they passed through a number of abandoned Catawba towns. Seeing them, Trotting Wolf was more convinced than ever before that he was pursuing the right course for his people.

At last they arrived at the Valley Town of the Catawbas. It was a large town, larger than Kituwah, and completely fenced in. Big Male Deer led the way into the town. As at Kituwah, the passageway made by the overlapping ends of the fence allowed only single-file entry.

After the initial excitement over the arrival of so many visitors, introductions were made and people were fed. Then Big Male Deer approached Trotting Wolf.

"My chief wants you to come to a meeting," he said.

"Good," answered Trotting Wolf. "There is much to talk about."

They met in the house of the chief, who was called the Big Catawba. Trotting Wolf, Big Male Deer, Little Black Bear and Jacques Tournier. They shook hands all around and then sat on the benches that lined the walls of the house. The Big Catawba filled a pipe with tobacco, lit it and passed it around. When the pipe was finished, he put it aside, leaned back, cleared his throat and started to speak.

"We're all here for one reason," he said. "To talk about these Spaniards who are trying to establish themselves in our land and have caused our people so much misery. I think for our friend the Chalakee, we should say from the beginning that the Frenchmen here are not like the Spanish. These Frenchmen are enemies of the Spanish, and they're our friends."

The Big Catawba had been speaking in the trade language for the benefit of Trotting Wolf. He paused to allow Little Black Bear to repeat what he had said in French.

"*Oui,*" said Tournier. "These Spanish are trying to take over your land. They want to govern, and they want to make slaves of all your people. We *Français* want only to establish trade relations with you. The Spanish don't want us in here. They want all this land for themselves. If you want to drive them out, we'll help you."

Little Black Bear translated what Tournier had said into the jargon, and Trotting Wolf and the Big Catawba both nodded their heads.

"They tell me," said the Big Catawba, "that there are two hundred of these Spaniards on the island. They have their big riding animals, and they have metal weapons. They even have the weapons that shoot fire and metal and make loud noises."

Again he paused, and again Little Black Bear translated. Then Tournier responded.

"There are twenty-five well-armed Frenchmen here," he said. "We also have guns."

Little Black Bear translated into the jargon.

"There are fifty of my men with me," said Trotting Wolf.

"From my town," said the Big Catawba, "we can get seventy-five or one hundred. That should be enough to attack the Spaniards. There may be other Catawbas from other Catawba towns too."

"Maybe a few scouts should go look at the island first," said Trotting Wolf. "They could come back and tell the rest what it's like, and we could make battle plans."

After hearing the translation, Tournier agreed. The Big Catawba declared it unanimous and said that it would be done. Trotting Wolf volunteered to be one of the scouts, as did Tournier. Little Black Bear then said that he, too, must go, for Trotting Wolf and Tournier would not be able to communicate with each other. The Big Catawba said that three would be enough.

"When will you leave?" he asked.

"In the morning," suggested Trotting Wolf.

The other two volunteers agreed, and so it was decided. The three scouts would leave for the island the following morning at the first appearance of the sun.

It was late night, and Father Tomás was snoring. 'Squani got up from his bed. He moved slowly and carefully so as not to awaken the priest. He pulled on his Spanish panalones and went outside. He stood there by the door for a moment to make sure that the priest was still asleep and that none of the soldiers were out and about. When he felt relatively safe, he moved to the door of the cabin in which Osa slept. He opened the door slightly.

"Osa," he said in a harsh whisper. "Osa. Are you awake?"

"Fortunato? Is that you?"

'Squani had spoken to her in Spanish, and she had answered him in that language. He continued with it.

"May I come in?"

"Yes," she said. "Of course."

'Squani pushed the door a little farther open and squeezed himself through sideways. Then he shut the door. It was so dark inside the hut that he couldn't see.

"You're getting to be pretty good with your Spanish," he said into the darkness, feeling a little foolish.

"Gracias," she said. "But I know so little."

"It takes time," said 'Squani.

"Do you want to come over here and sit beside me?"

"I can't see," said 'Squani. "My eyes aren't used to this darkness yet. That takes time, too."

She laughed, and he liked the sound of her laughter. He felt good that he had been able to bring at least a little happiness back into her life.

"I can bring you over," she said, switching to the trade language.

"All right," he said.

Osa walked over to his side and took him by the arm. A thrill went through his body at her touch.

"Come on," she said, and she led him across the room to

the bench—or bed—where she had been lying. They sat down side by side, and she did not let go of his arm. He was glad.

"I couldn't sleep," he said. "I thought that if you were also awake, we might talk."

"I'm glad you came," she said.

"Thank you."

'Squani wanted to put his arms around Osa and pull her close to him, but he did not want to seem to her like another of the rough soldiers. She moved closer to him and he felt her body against his. Still he made no move.

"You know," he said, "when the church is built, Father Tomás will baptize us, you and me. After that, if you're willing, I'd like to marry you. We'd be Christians. We could have a Christian marriage in the church."

"I'd like that too," she said, "except—"

"Except what?"

"What would we do after that?"

"Oh, I don't know. We might stay here on the island and work in the church with Father Tomás. Or we might go to Spain."

"I don't want to go to Spain. I don't want to be around Spaniards. I only want to be with you."

Father Tomás woke up feeling pressure on his bladder. He got out of bed and put on his gown. He felt for the staff which leaned against the wall. He always carried it with him when he walked about at night. He made his way outside and around behind the hut where he relieved himself. Then he headed back to bed.

As he opened the door to his hut, the bright moonlight

lit a small portion of the dark room. 'Squani was not in his bed. The priest almost ignored it. He looked again. 'Squani was gone. Father Tomás had only just then walked around the hut, and he had not seen 'Squani out there. There was no reason for him to be anywhere else in the middle of the night.

The priest turned away from the hut and looked out toward the middle of the compound. He saw no movement. He looked from one side to the other.

"Where," he said quietly and to no one but himself, "could he be?"

He walked rapidly toward the other end of the compound. He came to the fire that burned all night, the place where the sentry was on duty. The sentry was sitting on the ground leaning back against the wall of a hut. He scampered to his feet when he heard the approaching footsteps.

"Pablo," said the priest.

"*Padre,* what are you doing out so late?"

"Have you seen Fortunato?"

"Why, no. No one has been out tonight. Is something wrong?"

"No. No," said Father Tomás. "Never mind, Pablo."

He turned to head back toward his own hut but stopped and faced the sentry again.

"Let me have a torch, will you?"

"Of course," said the sentry. He walked to the fire and pulled a faggot from it. One end was blazing. He handed it to the *padre*.

"*Gracias,*" said Father Tomás, and, holding the torch up, hurried back toward his hut. Here and there he slowed down or stopped to peer around the dark corners of the small cabins, holding the torch out in front of him. He saw nothing.

Back at the door of his own hut, he hesitated. He turned and looked at the hut he had built for Osa. Perhaps, he thought, she had heard something. He hated to wake her, but he would ask her anyway. He stepped to her door and pushed it open. The light from his torch danced inside the dark hut, and there in its glimmer he saw the naked flesh of 'Squani, and underneath him was the woman.

SEVENTEEN

*P*UTA," Father Tomás shouted. "Filthy whore. And you, Fortunato."

'Squani turned his head to look over his shoulder, and he saw the priest, his face hideously twisted and contorted with rage in the flickering light. He saw the staff in the priest's right hand raised high over his head.

"Father," he said.

"I'll teach you. I'll beat the devil out of you."

The priest swung the staff down across the bare back of 'Squani. He swung it again and again. 'Squani took several blows, then, as he felt the sting, he turned. The staff rose again. 'Squani jumped up from the bench. He reached out and clutched the staff as it descended once more. He wrenched it from the hands of the enraged priest and struck out with one end, catching Father Tomás on the side of the head. The priest shouted out in pain, reached for his head with both hands and dropped to his knees. 'Squani turned frantically, grabbed up his pantalones and Osa's dress, then took Osa by an arm.

136

"Come on," he said. "Hurry."

They stepped around the groveling priest and out the door. The torch Father Tomás had been holding in his left hand had fallen against the wall, where its flames began to lick at the logs. As 'Squani and Osa ran around the hut into the darkness of the woods, Pablo, who had heard the commotion, came running toward the burning hut.

"Father," he called. "Father. What's happening?"

The priest came out of the hut on his hands and knees. The side of his head was covered with blood. Then Pablo saw the flames.

"Fire," he shouted. "Fire!"

"Let it burn," said the priest. "Go after them."

"After who, Father?" said Pablo.

Juan Sol came running up just then, two or three soldiers following behind him.

"Fortunato," said the priest. "Fortunato and his damned whore."

"Osa?" said Sol.

"Yes. Go after them. Hurry."

"It's no good in the dark, Father," said Juan Sol. "We'll look for them in the morning. Don't worry. We'll catch them. Right now we have to put out this fire. You men, bring buckets of water. Hurry up about it."

"The *padre* told me to let it burn," said Pablo.

"We can't take a chance on that," said Sol. "The flames might spread to the other cabins. Get going."

The soldiers, including Pablo, the sentry, ran for water, and Juan Sol dropped to one knee beside Father Tomás. He took the priest by his arm.

"Come on, Father," he said. "Let me help you. Come on."

Father Tomás allowed himself to be helped to his feet. His hands again went to his head.

"Come on, Father," said Sol. "We'll go to my cabin."

"They must be caught and punished," said the priest.

"Yes, *padre*. They will be. They can't go far in the darkness. We'll round them up in the morning. First thing. Then they'll be punished severely, according to your own wishes. Come along now. We have to take care of that wound on your head. What did he hit you with, Father?"

'Squani ran as fast as he could, holding on to Osa's arm, and she did not slow him. She kept up. She almost passed him once or twice. They ran into the woods down the path that they both knew, the path which led to the clear stream, expecting all the while to hear the horses' hooves, the shouts of the soldiers, the clanking of weapons, the baying of the vicious dogs behind them. They heard nothing, and they kept running.

At last, gasping for breath, they reached the stream. They stopped there, and at first they could do nothing but try to catch their breath. Finally, 'Squani, still panting, held Osa's dress out toward her.

"Here," he said. "Put it on."

She took it, and he pulled on his own pantalones. They had nothing else except the staff which 'Squani had taken from the priest.

"Are you all right?" he asked her.

"Yes," she said. "But how are you?"

"I'm all right. Let's go then. We can't stay here. We have to get off this island."

They walked into the water and then down the middle of

the stream toward the end of the island near the peninsula. The cold water felt good to their cut and bruised feet, and they hurried on as fast as they could walk in the water. Near the end of the island, they left the stream and walked to the point which was nearest the peninsula.

"We can walk across here," said 'Squani. "It's not deep."

He took her by the hand and they stepped into the salty seawater. The water lapped around their ankles. They took another step, and it was above their knees. The third step brought the water up to their waists, and 'Squani began to feel nervous. He tried to see the land across the way, but he could not. He took another step, and he felt no bottom. He lost the staff he carried, but he managed to hold on to Osa's hand.

They flailed in the water until they reached the surface again, and they gasped for air. 'Squani felt the saltwater burning the cuts on his back, but he was more concerned with keeping his head above water and with Osa's safety.

"Swim," he said.

"Let go of me," she said. "I can swim."

They swam into the darkness, hoping that they were swimming straight ahead toward the land at the tip of the peninsula, gasping for breath with every stroke. 'Squani could see nothing.

"Osa," he said. "Are you there?"

"Yes. Keep swimming."

And then they felt the sand beneath them. In another moment they were walking. They struggled a few steps through water chest deep. Then it was down to their waists. In a few more steps they walked out onto the sandy beach and collapsed side by side.

At last, breathing a little more easily, 'Squani rolled over onto his back. He rolled his head to the side to look at Osa lying there in the sand beside him.

"I don't understand it," he said. "I'm sure that's the same place I walked across before."

"The water goes up and down," said Osa.

"You mean, without rain, the water gets higher here?"

"Yes. All along the edge, where the saltwater is, it does that."

"I've never been to the big saltwater before," said 'Squani. Then, almost all at once, he began to feel the pain from the beating he had taken at the hands of the angry priest. He groaned out loud.

"Are you hurt?" asked Osa, her voice betraying obvious concern.

"Ah," said 'Squani. "It's the bruises where Father Tomás beat me."

"Did he do that because of—what we were doing?"

"Yes," said 'Squani. "I guess so. His big book says that it's a sin—unless two people are married to each other."

"But the soldiers did it with me. They made me do it."

'Squani sat up with a groan. He felt the pain shoot through his body.

"I don't understand the Christians," he said. "Father Tomás says that all the Spaniards are Christians. He says that we should be Christians too, and he says that certain things are sins. Yet the Spanish soldiers do all of those things, and no one punishes them for it."

"Will you go back?" she asked.

"No. I can't go back there now. Not after he beat me. Not after I hit him. No. I won't go back."

"But you said that you were a Spaniard, and you wanted to learn everything about being a Spaniard. You want to go to Spain."

"I know I said that, but I don't want that anymore. I don't know what I am. I don't know where to go. I only know that I want to be with you, but I shouldn't ask you to stay with me."

"Why not?" she said.

"Because I have no home. I have no place to take you. I should take you to your own people where you'll be safe."

"My village no longer exists," she said. "I have no home either."

"But you're a Catawba person. Your people will take you in somewhere."

She sat up then and stared at the sand there in front of her.

"I don't want to go to my people," she said, "unless you want to stay there with me."

"Well," said 'Squani, "let's go find some of your people then, and we'll see from there."

He stood up and held a hand toward her. She took it, and he pulled her to her feet.

"We should go now," he said. "In the morning, they'll probably come looking for us. We should get as far away as we can before then."

They walked most of that night, heading generally southwest. Osa said that there was a large Catawba town in that direction, one which she was fairly sure had not been touched by the Spaniards. The nearer towns, the ones to the west and the north, had almost all been destroyed. 'Squani knew about the ones to the west. He had come through them. He knew also about at least one to the north, for he had been there when the Spaniards attacked.

"But that one was Waccamaw," he said.

"The Waccamaw People are allies of my people," said Osa.

They stopped to rest, and 'Squani stayed awake while Osa slept. When she was awake again, he was ready to go.

"But you should sleep, too," she said. "I can watch."

"I'll sleep when we're farther away from the island," said 'Squani. "We're not traveling very fast in the dark, and when the Spaniards come after us, they'll be riding their *caballos*. They will catch up with us easily."

They moved on. 'Squani's back hurt more as the night wore on. He began to fear that one or two ribs had been cracked by the blows from the priest's staff. He also began to worry about being unarmed, and he thought about the sword he had left behind in the priest's hut. And he was hungry. He didn't say anything about his worries to Osa. She probably thought about the same things anyway, and if she didn't, why should he worry her?

When he saw the sun begin to light the eastern sky, he was a little relieved. He didn't know how far they had managed to get away from the island, but at least they could see where they were going, and they could see behind them in case of a pursuit.

"Over there is a river," said Osa, pointing a little to their left, to the southwest. "The big Valley Town is on that river."

'Squani could see the trees where they lined the river-bank.

"Let's go on down to it," he said. "Then we can follow

it to the town. We might even be able to find something to eat down there."

When they reached the river, they waded in to wash themselves and to allow the fresh water to ease their sore and aching muscles. Then they rested a short while to allow the sun to dry their bodies. Their Spanish-issue clothing looked a mess, but they washed it as well as they could in the river and laid it out to dry. Then Osa fashioned a bed of leaves and grass.

"That's for you," she said. "I'll watch while you sleep."

'Squani was too tired to protest, so he lay down, and he was asleep in a very short while. Osa walked to the edge of the trees where she could watch back over the prairie, the way they had come. She saw no pursuit, and she could see for a good distance. She started looking along the edge of the trees for edible plants.

A rabbit bounded away at her approach. Its first leap startled her. Watching its escape, she longed for a bow and arrows, a throwing stick even. Overhead a squirrel chattered, and again she wished for a weapon of some kind. She tried to put meat out of her mind and concentrate on the kind of food she could gather without weapons.

When 'Squani came out of his sleep, she was there beside him with a pile of greens and tubers.

"These are all good to eat," she said. "And no one is coming. Not near enough for me to see them anyway. Eat."

They ate, and the plant food took the sharp edge off their hunger. Then 'Squani went to the edge of the trees to look out across the prairie one more time. He saw no one coming, so he went back to the river where Osa was waiting.

"There are squirrels and rabbits here," she said, "and fish in the river, but we have no way to get them."

"Let's get a little farther away," said 'Squani. "Then we'll find a way."

EIGHTEEN

JUAN SOL was reluctant to take too many soldiers away from the outpost at one time. In spite of Father Tomás's ravings, he decided that a troop of six, himself and five others, would be enough. After all, they were only chasing two *Indios,* and one of them was a woman. And as far as he knew, they were not only unarmed, but practically naked.

"How much trouble can they give us, Father?" he asked rhetorically. "Two naked *Indios? * All we have to do is find them and bring them back to you."

Father Tomás gave a shrug.

"Have an extra horse saddled, Juan," he said. "I'm riding with you."

"Padre," said Sol, "do you think that's wise?"

"After all," repeated Father Tomás, "how much trouble can they give us?"

"All right, *padre.* I'll have a horse saddled for you. We'll be ready to ride almost immediately."

"You won't have to wait for me," said the priest. "I'm ready to go."

He ducked quickly back into his hut. There, standing in a corner of the room near the head of the bed that had been 'Squani's, was the sword that Marcos Zavala had given the young man. Father Tomás picked it up and strapped it on around his waist. Just two *Indios,* he thought scornfully. These were two very important *Indios.* His first two converts, and they had shamed him. It was a matter of pride. They had to be caught and punished, and they had to be punished publicly. He buckled the belt on. Then he went back outside and headed for the other end of the compound, where they would be getting the horses ready. He was conscious of curious, even startled, eyes upon him, the armed *padre.*

Juan Sol was shouting orders when he saw the priest returning. He noticed the sword immediately. It didn't seem proper to him for the priest to be armed, nor did it seem necessary. There were already six fully armed soldiers going after the two naked savages. He chose to keep those thoughts to himself, however. The priest was in an angry mood, and Sol did not want to antagonize him.

He looked back at the horses. They were saddled and ready to go. Pablo Trancoso was there with the extra horse.

"Pablo," called Sol, "bring the *padre* his *caballo.*"

Trancoso led the horse over to Father Tomás and helped the priest up into the saddle. Sol ordered the five soldiers to mount up and left Trancoso in charge of the outpost during his absence. Then, with a shout and a wave of his arm, he started the small column moving. Father Tomás rode alongside Sol at the head of the column.

They rode the length of the island and crossed to the peninsula in a short time. There they found evidence in the sand that the two fugitives had also crossed there. They followed the tracks as far as they could, but when the open beach ended at the edge of the woods, the tracks disappeared.

"They seem to be headed southwest," said Sol. "We'll go on that way and see if we can spot them or find their tracks again."

They rode through the woods and came out on the prairie. There they could see across to the tree-lined river valley. There was no sign of the two escapees.

"They must have gone on to that river valley there," said Father Tomás.

"*Sí,*" said Sol. "I think so too. There's no place else for them to go. Come on. Let's ride."

And so they headed toward the river, riding hard.

'Squani and Osa walked along the edge of the river, still moving generally southwest. They were still hungry, but they did not feel safe enough yet to take time to find a way to hunt or fish. They kept moving.

"Wait for me here," said 'Squani. "I want to look out across the prairie again."

He made his way through the trees to the other side and swept the landscape with his gaze. Something moved out there. It was on the far horizon. He waited and watched. It seemed like a long wait, but then he could see that there were mounted men. The Spaniards were coming after them. He had begun to hope that the pursuit would not be so persistent, would not follow them so far, but he could see the Spaniards coming.

They seemed a long way off yet, but he knew that the horses could move fast. He waited a little longer. There were seven of them. He decided that he had taken enough time, and he hurried back through the trees to where Osa waited by the river.

"They're coming," he said. "Seven of them."

"Do they know where we are?"

"They're headed in our direction," he said. "By the time the sun goes down, I think they'll catch us."

"What should we do?"

"We have no weapons," he said. "There are seven of them, and they're mounted. We can't fight them. We have to run or hide. I think we should turn around and follow the river east."

"But that will take us away from the Valley Town," she said.

"Yes, but it will take us away from the Spaniards too," said 'Squani. "If we can keep them from finding us for a long enough time, maybe they'll give up and go back to the island. Then we can go on to the Valley Town. It will take us longer to get there, but we'll be safer."

She thought for a moment before she answered.

"You're right, Fortunato," she said. "We'll go east. They won't think to look for us in that direction."

'Squani stood silent for a moment.

"I'm not Fortunato," he said. "The *padre* named me that. The name I grew up with is Asquani. It means Spaniard in the language of the Real People. I would rather be called 'Squani."

Just then they were startled by the sudden appearance of a dugout canoe coming from the west. There were three men in the canoe, and they seemed to be as startled by the sight of 'Squani and Osa standing there beside the river as were the two fugitives. Then 'Squani recognized the three men.

"It's all right," he said to Osa. "I know them." Then he waved. "Trotting Wolf," he called out.

The three men brought the canoe to land and stepped out.

"You're 'Squani, aren't you?" asked Trotting Wolf, his face betraying his astonishment at seeing this young man from Kituwah so far away from home. He had spoken in the language of the Real People.

"Yes, I am, and you're Trotting Wolf. This is Osa. She's a Catawba, and she's been a captive of the Spaniards. I too was with the Spaniards, but we ran away last night." Then he turned to Osa, and he shifted from the language of the Real People to the trade language. "This is Trotting Wolf from my town, and these two I met on the road. I don't remember their names, but this one is not a Spaniard. He's another kind of white man."

"He's a Frenchman, an enemy of the Spaniards," said Little Black Bear, "and he's my friend. I'm a Catawba from Valley Town. I'm called Little Black Bear."

Translations were made back and forth until everyone had been properly introduced and the three scouts from the Valley Town all understood where 'Squani and Osa had come from.

"We've been sent from Valley Town to look over the island where the Spanish are staying," said Little Black Bear. "We plan to attack it and kill all the Spaniards."

"There are seven of them just over there," said 'Squani, and he pointed toward the prairie on the other side of the trees. "They're chasing us, and they're riding the big animals."

"Can the four of us kill them?" asked Little Black Bear.

"There are five of us here," said Osa. "But we two have no weapons."

There was more discussion and more translation, and then Trotting Wolf spoke in the trade language.

"We have weapons enough for all," he said. He glanced at 'Squani. "Can you show me where they are?"

"Yes," said 'Squani. "Follow me."

He led Trotting Wolf through the trees to the prairie's edge and pointed. The riders had moved well down below the horizon. Trotting Wolf watched them for a moment.

"All right," he said. "Come on."

They rejoined the others, and Trotting Wolf called them all together.

"I saw them," he said. "Seven. They are coming this way, but we have time to get ready for them. I think we should take them here. That will be seven fewer of them for the big fight."

"Yes," said Osa.

Tournier and Little Black Bear agreed. 'Squani sat silent, but his silence was taken as agreement.

"Good," said Trotting Wolf. "Let's decide how we'll do this thing."

The line of trees in the river valley was just ahead, and Juan Sol halted his little column.

"Why are we stopping here?" demanded Father Tomás. He burned to get his hands on his backsliding converts.

"Please, *padre*," said Sol. He sat for a moment in silence, studying the trees. "They probably went in there," he said. "I've heard that there's a big town on this river farther to the southwest. I bet that they're following the river to that town."

"Yes, that's logical," said Father Tomás. "It's probably

exactly what they're doing. So what are we waiting for? If they get to the town, we'll have to turn around and go back for more men."

"Just to be careful, Father," said Sol. "Just to be sure that we know what we're doing."

"They're only two," said the priest, "and one of them is a woman."

"Yes, I know," said Juan Sol, and he thought, why then did you feel the need to join us and arm yourself? Juan Sol fancied himself to be a religious man, especially for a soldier. He had always thought that Zavala failed to show the proper respect for Father Tomás, but now even Sol was beginning to wonder about this priest, this man of God who rode out in a rage, wearing a sword. Sol looked back over his shoulder toward the soldiers while pointing toward the trees ahead and to his right. "Diego," he said, "go down there and ride along the edge of the trees. Look along that way."

"Sí, Sargento," said Diego, "but what will I be looking for?"

"Just look. See what you can see. Maybe some sign of where they went into the woods? Maybe something like that? Now get going." He pointed with his left hand in the other direction. "Baltasar, you look that way."

The two riders urged their mounts toward the trees and rode slowly in opposite directions close along the edge. Soon Baltasar stopped. He leaned over in his saddle for a closer look at the ground. He dismounted and squatted there for a moment, studying something intently. Then he stood up, turned back toward where Sol waited, put a hand to the side of his mouth, and shouted.

"*Sargento,* over here. I've found something over here, I think."

"*Silencio, bobo,*" said Juan Sol. "If anyone's in there, they've heard that for sure. Now we've lost all chance of surprising them. Ah, well, come on then. Come on then."

He led the others on down to where Baltasar waited, and he dismounted and walked over to join Baltasar. He looked at the ground there where the soldier stood. As he neared, Baltasar squatted again and pointed.

"Right here, *Sargento,*" he said. "Do you see? Do you think that this is the place?"

"*Sí, observo,*" said Sol. "Someone has gone through here recently. The grass and the brush are trampled down almost to a footpath. It's still too thick here, though, to ride the *caballos* through. Dismount and leave them here. Secure them well."

The soldiers all got down out of their saddles and tied their horses to trees. Juan Sol drew his sword, and the others, including Father Tomás, did the same. Then Sol lifted his arm, made a forward sweeping motion and stepped into the trees. Father Tomás was right behind him. The others followed. They went into the woods single file, Juan Sol, Father Tomás, Baltasar Mendoza, Carlos Bustillas, Pedro Valdéz, Martín Morales and Diego Pacheco. They marched toward the river.

NINETEEN

THEY had planned it carefully. A man could be killed easily, with a stick, a rock, with bare hands. But there was value in shock, and so they planned it for shock, to surprise and startle, to momentarily disorient. The Spaniards were in pursuit of two runaways, supposedly unarmed and helpless. Instead there were five waiting in ambush for them, five to kill seven. They were outnumbered. The initial shock was crucial to the plan.

They watched Juan Sol fight his way down the narrow path, brushing limbs away from his face with his arm, hacking at vines and brush with his sword, and then at last stepping free, out of the tangle, only to find that he was looking into the barrel of Jacques Tournier's gun, his *tromblon,* or blunderbuss. The last thing Juan Sol saw was the flash. The last thing he heard was the roar. His final sensation was the acrid smell of burning powder. He made no sound. He fell backward heavily and landed with a clank and a thud.

Father Tomás looked down with horror at the red mass where Juan Sol's face should have been. He looked up, trying desperately to see through to the clearing, to see who it was who had made such a mess of Juan Sol's face. He could see that someone was out there. He could tell that it was not one of his runaway Christian *Indios.* He thought that he could see a white man, a European, but there was something wrong with the clothing. It was not Spanish. Something was amiss. Then he knew. For a moment, he stood there, his mouth hanging open, trying to shout. At last a word formed itself and seemingly of its own volition burst forth to freedom.

"Francés," he shouted.

As soon as he heard the blast of Tournier's gun, Trotting Wolf stepped out of his hiding place in the trees. He came up behind Diego Pacheco. He knew what he had to do. He knew about the Spanish armor. He reached around with his left hand to cover the mouth and nose of Pacheco and to pull back the head. Then with his right he ripped at the exposed throat with the jagged blade of his flint knife.

Pacheco, too, died without a sound. Blood gushing from his throat, he collapsed against the body of his killer. Trotting Wolf stepped back, allowing the body to lie on its back in the path. The first and the last were down.

The five in the middle began shouting orders at each other and looking around for someone to fight. Martín Morales looked back over his shoulder and saw the dead Pacheco behind him, and behind the body, he saw Trotting Wolf holding the bloody knife. He turned in the path, intent on leaping over the body and attacking the *Indio* there, his long steel sword against the other's short flint knife.

An arrow came out of the woods to his left, and it drove itself through his neck. He staggered, making ghastly gurgling sounds, and then, suddenly he sat down, the way a toddler sits, by falling backward and landing on his rump. He stayed there in a sitting position, his legs poking out straight in front of him, the arrow all the way through his neck, the tipped end nasty with his blood. Then slowly, almost deliberately, he lay back. One hand went up to his neck, but it did not touch the deadly missile lodged there.

From behind a tree beside the path, Osa nocked another arrow. Just ahead of Morales in line, Pedro Valdéz turned around. He saw Morales lying there, saw the shaft protruding from both sides of the neck, saw Morales's eyes rolling in his head. It was painfully obvious to Valdéz that the attack was coming from at least three sides. He still saw no attackers, but Pacheco and Morales were both down behind him, the gunshot had come from up ahead and the arrow had been shot from the side.

Valdéz stood braced for action, his sword in his right hand, a knife in his left. He looked from one side to the other. He turned to face one end of the path, then turned again to face the other.

"Wherever you are," he shouted, "come out and fight."

Little Black Bear stepped into the path holding a long wooden lance tipped with flint. He was standing behind Valdéz. Valdéz turned again, shouted at the sight of the *Indio* and raised his sword. Little Black Bear's aim was careful and deliberate. He bent his knees in order to make an upward thrust from a low position. The tip of the lance entered Valdéz's body just below his belt buckle. It ran upward through the stomach, chipped a lower rib at the back and was stopped by the armor. The power of Little Black Bear's thrust almost lifted Valdéz off his feet. The Catawba released his grip on the lance, and Valdéz slowly leaned forward. He dropped to his knees, then tilted forward again only to be stopped in his movement when the opposite end of the lance dug itself into the ground. Then, at last, Valdéz fell over to the side.

As soon as he had discharged his gun into the face of Juan Sol, Jacques Tournier had tossed the gun aside and whipped out his sword. When the turmoil from behind got the full attention of Baltasar Mendoza, he hurried forward, but he ran into the back of the frantic priest. He put a hand on the *padre*'s back and shoved.

"Move on out of here, Father," he shouted. "They're killing us from behind."

Father Tomás ran ahead of Mendoza. He nearly stumbled over the body of Juan Sol, but he managed to come out of the woods standing on his feet. When Tournier saw the two men emerge from the narrow path, he backed away slowly toward the water's edge.

"Ah," he said, "two of you. The day I can't take two Spaniards, I'm ready to die. Come on, you dogs, *salauds.*"

"Move to your left, Father," said Mendoza, as he himself was easing to the right.

"There are others behind us," said the priest.

"Then turn and face them. I'll handle this Frenchman."

Father Tomás turned to look back down the path as Mendoza and Tournier crossed blades. Then 'Squani stepped out of the woods. He held in his hand a ball-headed war club.

"Fortunato," said the priest.

"No. I'm Asquani. You shouldn't have beat me, Father. I was yours until that moment."

The priest raised his sword up over his head.

"And you're mine still," he said.

But before he could swing the weapon, Osa stepped into the path. She drew back the string of her bow and released the arrow. It struck Father Tomás just below the sternum, driving itself in deep. The priest stood for a moment, arm still high, a startled expression on his face. He looked down at the offending missile which protruded from his body. His hand relaxed, and the sword fell to the ground behind him. Then he dropped to his knees. Both hands reached to clutch the arrow. He looked up with pleading eyes.

"Fortunato?" he said.

'Squani stepped forward and looked down into the eyes

of the priest. "Asquani," he said, and he bashed in the head of the priest with his club.

Back on the path, Little Black Bear and Trotting Wolf busied themselves by making sure that those lying wounded were actually dead. When they had finished their grisly work and made their way down the path to the river-bank, they found 'Squani and Osa watching fascinated as the two Europeans dueled with swords. They squatted side by side to observe.

"Should we kill the Spaniard?" asked 'Squani.

"I think Jacques Tournier is doing well enough," said Little Black Bear.

"Let's just watch this," said Trotting Wolf. "At least for a while. I've never seen this kind of fighting before."

The two swordsmen seemed to be evenly matched. When one would thrust, the other would parry. Back and forth they moved along the edge of the water, the swords clanking as they fought. Then the Spaniard took a mighty sideways swipe aimed at the head of the Frenchman. 'Squani and the others gasped out loud as Tournier bent his knees and ducked below the whistling blade just in time. It sliced the plume on his hat in half. Mendoza backed away a little. He glanced at the small audience watching there, and then he looked back at Tournier. He knew he was alone.

"This is a fine setup for you," he said. "If I kill you, they kill me."

"Qu'est-ce qu'il y a?" said Tournier, glancing toward Little Black Bear and 'Squani for help. The Catawba trans-lated the French for 'Squani, then 'Squani gave a quick translation of what the Spaniard had said. Tournier held up his left hand to ask for a pause in the fight. "Tell him for

me, please," he said, "that if he should be so lucky as to kill me, none of you will touch him. You'll let him go free. Tell him that."

Again Little Black Bear translated the French, this time into the trade language. Trotting Wolf looked at the others. They shrugged nonchalantly.

"Tell him we agree," said Trotting Wolf.

"We have promised our friend, the Frenchman," said 'Squani, speaking Spanish, "that if you kill him, we'll let you live. We'll keep our promise."

"Well then," said Mendoza, glaring at Tournier, "have at you."

Mendoza rushed at Tournier with renewed fury born of hope. All he had to do to live was to kill one foppish Frenchman. He slashed and he hacked, and Tournier parried all of his blows. Then suddenly and unexpectedly the Frenchman's blade sliced the forearm of the Spaniard.

"Ah."

Mendoza vocalized his pain and surprise as his sword fell to the ground. He looked down as if he meant to reach for it, but the tip of Tournier's blade was just there at his chest, high up near his throat. His eyes lifted to look into the face of the Frenchman. Beads of perspiration ran down his forehead.

"Por favor," he said, *"cómo se llama?"*

Tournier understood that much Spanish. He smiled.

"Jacques Tournier," he said, and he ran the blade of his sword into the Spaniard's throat.

They gathered up the swords and knives from the Spanish bodies, 'Squani taking the sword from the remains of

Father Tomás. It had been his anyway, and he strapped the belt on around his waist.

"Where are we going now?" asked Little Black Bear.

"We were going to the island for a look," said Trotting Wolf.

"For what purpose?" asked 'Squani.

"So we can describe it to the others," said Trotting Wolf. "So we can plan the way to attack."

"I can describe the island," said 'Squani. "I and Osa. We lived there."

"That's right," said Little Black Bear. "There's no need now for us to go on to the island. We can go right back to Valley Town and make our plans. If these two will go with us."

"We were going there anyway," said 'Squani.

"De quoi s'agit-il?" said Tournier.

Little Black Bear summarized the conversation in French for him, and Tournier nodded his agreement.

"Bien," he said. *"Très bien."*

"For now," said Trotting Wolf, "we should camp, but not here with these dead Spaniards. We can all ride in the canoe. It's a big one."

"We can ride the big animals, too," said 'Squani.

Trotting Wolf looked at him for a moment, perplexed.

"We don't know how to ride those *sogwilis*," he said.

"I know how. I could show you. And the Frenchman. He probably knows how. There are seven of them there. We should take them with us."

After some discussion involving translations back and forth, it was at last decided that Tournier and 'Squani would ride horses. They would lead the extra mounts along. The others would ride back to Valley Town in the canoe. That way they would get the horses and save time. Teaching the others to ride would take time.

The sun was low in the western sky, and so they moved on toward Valley Town, until they felt they had gotten far enough away from the scene of the fight for comfort. 'Squani and Tournier brought the horses. The others went by water. Then they camped beside the river for the night. They did not think that more Spaniards would be coming along, but to be safe, one stood watch through the night. They would go on to Valley Town the next day.

TWENTY

'SQUANI lay awake that night beside Osa. Her arm was across his chest, and he thought that her touch was pleasant, but his thoughts were troubled. He had left the Real People because he had not felt at home among them. He had felt isolated and alone, in spite of the fact that he had been born in Kituwah. He had no clan and therefore, he believed, he had never really been accepted as one of the Real People. He had longed for the company of the people of his unknown and mysterious Spanish father, and so he had gone to the island where the Spaniards were building their outpost.

He had tried to be Spanish, and he had learned a great deal. He could speak the language with any Spaniard. He knew the Christian stories. He had even learned to read Spanish a little. He had actually read from the big book, from *La Biblia*. And all the while he had tried to explain away the stories of Spanish cruelty that he had heard from

Deadwood Lighter and others.

But he had seen the cruelty. He had seen that side of the Spaniards for himself, and there was no denying it any longer. He had seen innocent people slaughtered and tortured and tormented, and he himself had felt the blows. And for no reason.

Among the Real People, what he had done with Osa was simply considered to be normal behavior. And he knew that the Spaniards felt the same way, for he knew what the soldiers had been doing with the women they held as slaves. The Spaniards felt the same way, except for Father Tomás. Yet even Father Tomás had not beaten the soldiers for the time they had spent with the women. Why then had he thrashed 'Squani so violently?

He did not understand the Spanish behavior, but he had learned enough to know that he would never be a Spaniard. He had been wrong about that particular desire. He wondered, though, if he had really experienced the life of a Spaniard, and somehow he did not think so. Among the Spanish he had been as he had among the Real People. He had not really been accepted as one of them. Would baptism have made a difference? Now he would never know, but he didn't really think so anyway.

He had left the Real People to go to the Spaniards. Now he had left the Spaniards, but he had no place to go. Osa had suggested that he live with her in the Catawba Valley Town, but there he would be an outsider too. At last, he drifted off to sleep with those unhappy thoughts in his troubled mind.

They were up with the sun and ready to go. There was not

much to pack. 'Squani and Tournier saddled the horses. The canoe was loaded. They were about to separate into their two parties when Osa took hold of 'Squani's arm.

"I want to go with you," she said. "I can ride the big animals."

"Then come on," said 'Squani. He smiled broadly. It was comforting to him to know that someone really wanted him, and he told himself that he was indeed lucky to have found this woman. In fact, he thought, it was worth all the time he had spent with the Spaniards, the beating he had suffered at the hands of Father Tomás and the fight at the river, just to have found her.

Trotting Wolf and Little Black Bear climbed into the dugout, and 'Squani and Tournier gave them a shove. As the dugout slid through the water, its occupants waved back over their shoulders at their companions.

"You can have your *sogwilis,* 'Squani," Trotting Wolf shouted. "We'll be in Valley Town before you."

'Squani laughed.

"We'll see, Trotting Wolf," he called out. "We'll see."

"Venez," said Jacques Tournier, and he added a gesture to make his meaning clear.

'Squani and Osa followed him to where the horses waited patiently. 'Squani took up the reins of one of the animals and handed them to Osa. She took them, put a foot in a stirrup and swung herself up into the saddle. 'Squani then mounted another of the horses. Tournier was already in the saddle. He held the reins of two of the riderless horses, and 'Squani took those of the remaining two. Then he looked at Osa.

"Watch me," he said. "This is how you make him go."

He gave her a quick lesson in the basics of handling a horse, and then they were on their way. For a while they rode along beside the trees, but soon they found themselves on higher ground. They could look over the tops of the trees and see the river winding along below.

"Regardez," said Jacques Tournier, and he was pointing to a bend in the river slightly ahead of them.

'Squani followed the gesture with his eyes, and he saw the dugout down below. He laughed and looked at Osa riding along beside him. She smiled back and nodded her head. She had seen it too. Then it was gone around the bend and hidden by the trees again.

"Maybe they *will* be there before us," 'Squani said.

The riding was good. It made him feel free, and it made him forget the things that had been bothering him. The strength and movement of the horse beneath him, the wind in his face and the woman riding along beside him all combined to make him feel that everything about life was good.

They stopped once to eat, and then they rode again. They did not see the dugout again. They talked little. By the middle of the afternoon, they saw the town ahead of them. Tournier was again the first to speak, and as usual, he accompanied his speech with a gesture. He stretched out his right arm to point straight ahead toward the town.

"Nous arrivons à la destination, mes amis," he said.

'Squani looked at Osa.

"Is that Valley Town?" he asked.

"Yes. That's it."

When they rode into Valley Town, the dogs barked and yapped at the horses. Children ran to see the strange, big animals with people on their backs. It seemed as if the entire population of the town was out in the streets, and all of them were shouting and laughing at the same time. And 'Squani could see among them large numbers of white men. Frenchmen, he said to himself.

Jacques Tournier, leading the way into the town, waved and smiled as he rode on through the crowd. He continued until he came up in front of the large townhouse, and there he stopped. 'Squani and Osa rode up beside him. They all dismounted. People crowded in to get a better look at the horses, but none got too close to the big animals.

Then 'Squani saw, standing in front of the doorway to the townhouse, their arms folded across their chests, wide grins on their faces, Trotting Wolf and Little Black Bear.

"Are you here at last, little brother?" said Trotting Wolf. "We had almost given up on ever seeing you again."

'Squani wondered at the way in which Trotting Wolf had addressed him, but he dismissed it. He's probably just being familiar because we've come through a fight together, he thought.

"Well," he said, "you were right. What can I say? You're here ahead of us. If we had made a bet, you'd have won."

"I thought about making a bet," said Trotting Wolf. "I should have."

The people of Valley Town fed the travelers, and then there was a big meeting in the townhouse. The Big Catawba presided. He announced the purpose of the meeting and reminded the people of the journey that Jacques Tournier and the others had undertaken and of the reason for that journey. He declared the undying friendship of the Catawba People and the French, and he loudly pro-

163

claimed a new but fast friendship for the "Chalakees." He explained that everything that would be said in the meeting that night would be repeated until it had been said in three languages: Catawba, the trade language and French. That way, he said, everyone would understand everything.

Then Little Black Bear told the story of the journey. He told his audience how he and his companions, on their way to look over the island of the Spaniards, had come upon Asquani and Osa, and how the five of them had ambushed the Spanish soldiers who were in pursuit of those two.

"That's how we got the big animals that you saw," he said.

And then the weapons they had taken from the dead Spaniards were displayed for all to see. And Little Black Bear explained that they had not gone on to the island because they had among them two who had lived there and could describe it well.

By the end of the evening, it had been decided that an all-out assault on the Spanish outpost would be undertaken. The Big Catawba announced that four days of fasting, dancing and singing would follow in preparation for war, and he added that there would be another meeting, a smaller one involving just the war leaders. It would take place sometime during the fasting. At that meeting 'Squani and Osa would describe the island to the others and tell them how many Spaniards they could expect to encounter. The battle plans would be laid at this meeting.

'Squani stood aside from the dancing. He fasted, and he stayed away from Osa, his woman, the way he should, but he did not dance. The other Real People did. They danced with the Catawbas who were preparing for war. Even a few of the Frenchmen danced with them. 'Squani did not.

He was standing next to one of the houses watching when Trotting Wolf approached him. 'Squani nodded to acknowledge the approach of the famous leader of the Wolves of the Real People.

" 'Squani," said Trotting Wolf, "at last we have time to talk, you and I."

"Yes," said 'Squani, and he was surprised to find that it really felt good to speak the language of the Real People again.

"You know," said Trotting Wolf, "I knew about it when you left Kituwah. We already had Wolves watching the passes, and they saw you go. We talked about you."

"What did you say?" asked 'Squani.

"Your parents were worried, but we all said that you would come back home when you were ready. I did wonder where you were going though. And when I came down here to this Catawba town, I didn't expect to find you."

"You found me running away from the Spaniards," said 'Squani.

"Yes," said Trotting Wolf, and he laughed. "And with a woman."

'Squani smiled.

"Yes," he said. "She's going to be my wife, Trotting Wolf."

"Oh? Good. She's a good woman. And she can fight. She killed two of those *Ani-'squani* herself, didn't she?"

"Yes, she did. The two that were killed with arrows. She shot them both."

"Well, well. Your parents will be surprised when you come home with a wife. They'll be happy to see you. They don't know yet even where you went. All they know is that you went away without telling them anything."

'Squani suddenly felt that Trotting Wolf was trying to get him to explain his behavior, and he began to wish that the Wolf would go away and leave him alone. He had no intention of explaining himself to anyone.

"So. Your wife is a Catawba woman, isn't she?" said Trotting Wolf. "Is this her town?"

"No," said 'Squani. "Her town was destroyed by the *Ani-'squani.*"

"Oh, that's too bad. A Catawba woman. We'll have to find her a clan when we get back to Kituwah."

'Squani looked at Trotting Wolf questioningly.

"A clan for Osa?" he said.

"Yes. Of course. How else can one be a Real Person? Of course, it can't be the Wolf Clan. Not if you really mean to marry this woman."

'Squani wondered if Trotting Wolf had gone crazy. He knew that he didn't want to listen to any more of the man's nonsense.

"What are you talking about?" he said.

"What?" said Trotting Wolf. "Oh. Of course. You were already gone, so you couldn't know about it."

"About what?"

"Your mother has been made a Wolf Person, and so you, too, of course, are now a Wolf."

TWENTY-ONE

THE French had a few horses, and 'Squani and his new companions had brought the seven Spanish horses back with them to the Catawba Valley Town. When they marched out headed for the island, the army was led by the Big Catawba, Trotting Wolf, Jacques Tournier, 'Squani and Osa. They were all mounted. Trotting Wolf rode uncomfortably, but he rode. Had he insisted on walking, he would not have been able to go as one of the leaders. So grudgingly, he rode.

Right behind the leaders rode the French cavalry, a small troop, and behind them the larger body of French foot soldiers. All together, there were forty Frenchmen. Behind them came around seventy Catawbas, and finally the fifty Real People who had followed Trotting Wolf from Kituwah.

It was a good-sized army, and 'Squani rode proudly at the head of it. He was riding a Spanish horse that he had won in battle. On his right rode the woman who would be his wife, a proud and brave Catawba woman, and on his left rode Trotting Wolf, one of the most famous warriors of the Real People and 'Squani's new kinsman.

It was a good strong army, well armed and eager to fight. Most of the Frenchmen had guns. The mounted French had lances. All wore swords. The Catawbas and the Real People were armed with bows and arrows, knives, and war clubs. Some carried spears.

'Squani was confident. They were well armed, and they were all ready and anxious to fight and to drive the hated

Spaniards out of the country. It had also occurred to 'Squani that the Spaniards would not be expecting an attack from a force of this size. So far they had met with little resistance. Usually people had run, leaving empty villages for them to plunder and burn. This attack would be unexpected.

And the Spaniards might be without effective leadership. After the death of Zavala, Juan Sol had become the leader, and now Juan Sol was dead. They might not even know of his death back at the island. That uncertainty might have them confused and undisciplined. And finally, 'Squani thought, the Spaniards on the island, so far as he knew, were not aware of the presence of the French.

'Squani was right. On the island, most of the Spanish soldiers were drunk or working diligently toward that end. They had all relaxed a little with the death of Zavala, but Juan Sol had been working hard to show them that he could take command. But with Sol off on an excursion, no one was able to take charge of things. Pablo Trancoso tried.

"I'm supposed to be in command in the absence of Juan Sol," he said.

"Who the hell told you that?" asked Silvio Chacón, a soldier with a wine bottle in his hand. "I never heard nobody tell you that."

"Juan Sol told me when he left. 'Take charge in my absence,' he said."

"Well," said Chacón, "I don't believe it when I don't hear it for myself. Besides, if anyone here should take charge, it should be me. I have more time and experience.

The men would follow me to the mouth of hell. They wouldn't follow you to a whorehouse."

"You're under arrest for insubordination," shouted Trancoso. "Give me your sword and confine yourself to quarters."

Chacón threw back his head and roared with laughter, and a couple of other soldiers who had been listening to the argument joined him. Trancoso's face grew red with rage.

"I demand some order here," he shouted. "I require respect for my office."

"He demands," said Chacón. "He requires. I require his pantalones."

The other laughing, drunken soldiers wrestled Trancoso to the ground, while he shouted oaths and threats. Chacón stepped up to stand over the struggling Trancoso.

"Have a drink," he said, "and calm yourself down."

He poured wine out of his bottle onto Trancoso's face. Trancoso sputtered and spat. Then Chacón tossed his bottle aside and unfastened Trancoso's trousers.

"I'll kill you for this," shouted Trancoso.

Chacón pulled at Trancoso's trousers, getting them down around the would-be commander's ankles. Then he fell over laughing in the dirt. He got up on his hands and knees to crawl over for the bottle where he had tossed it aside. The others rolled over laughing, and Trancoso struggled to his feet, his trousers still down around his ankles. He hopped up and down trying to maintain his balance.

"You're all under arrest," he said. "Damn you. I'm going for my sword, Chacón. Prepare yourself, Chacón. Defend yourself or die."

He hopped toward his hut, reaching down for his trousers as he hopped. He fell once, got up again and made it to the hut, disappearing inside.

Chacón was sitting on the ground drinking from his bottle. One of his companions in mischief staggered toward him.

"Silvio," he said, "Pablo has gone for his sword."

Chacón lurched to his feet, took another drink, shoved the bottle at the other man and drew his sword.

"It's too bad he can't take a joke," he said. "I guess that will be the death of him."

Trancoso stepped out the doorway of his hut. His left hand clutched the waistband of his trousers, his right held a sword.

"Chacón," he shouted.

Chacón turned to face Trancoso. For a tense moment, both men stood silent and defiant. Then, almost as if by some prearranged signal of which no one else was aware, they moved toward one another. One step. Another.

"Wait," shouted the other soldier. "Wait. I hear the horses. Juan Sol is coming back."

The two swordsmen turned away from each other to face the direction of the approach to the compound. They and the other two soldiers waited, quietly expectant. The sound of the horses' hooves grew louder. Then suddenly horsemen burst into view, and they were riding hard toward the middle of the compound.

"That's not Juan Sol," shouted Chacón.

Three riders were *Indios*. The others were French.

"To arms. To arms," shouted Trancoso.

"It's the French," shouted Chacón. "Hurry."

Men came out of the huts, some pulling on their clothes or strapping on their sword belts. Some were staggering from too much wine. And the horsemen were inside the compound, slashing with their swords. 'Squani cut down Pablo Trancoso with one stroke. Jacques Tournier slashed Silvio Chacón.

Trotting Wolf, glad to have reached his destination, jumped down off the back of the horse he had been riding. He raced at one of the other soldiers, brandishing his war club. The wretched soldier, who had just come out of his hut and was only half dressed, turned to run, and Trotting Wolf bashed his skull from behind.

Then the French foot soldiers came rushing in, and right behind them, the Catawbas and the Real People. The Spaniards were overwhelmed. Caught by surprise, many of them drunk or half drunk, they were unarmed or hastily and minimally armed.

The battle was over and done almost as soon as it had started, but there were five Spanish soldiers who ran from the compound unharmed. They ran through the woods to the far side of the island, and there they climbed into a boat which they kept for the purpose of rowing out to meet their ships when they arrived with supplies. When the fight within the compound was clearly over, one of the French soldiers ran over to Jacques Tournier.

"There are some yet alive," he said. "I saw them run that way."

Tournier and the soldier followed them. 'Squani, Trotting Wolf, Little Black Bear and a few others ran after them. When they reached the water's edge, they saw the boat. It was but a little ways out, still an easy bow shot.

They could hear the voices of the Spaniards, who looked back in fear and panic. Trotting Wolf held up a hand.

"Let them go," he said. "Let them tell their friends what happened to them here."

After 'Squani repeated the words in the trade language and Little Black Bear repeated them in French, everyone agreed. They stood there for a while and watched the last of the Spaniards recede in the distance.

"They may never reach their friends anyway," Tournier said in a low voice. *"On ne sait jamais."*

After setting fire to the Spanish outpost, the entire victorious army returned to the Valley Town of the Catawbas. They took with them all the weapons they could carry and all of the healthy Spanish horses. The former slaves of the Spaniards, mostly Catawbas, were also, of course, freed and taken along.

The next several days in Valley Town were spent in celebration and resting. Then Trotting Wolf and the other Real People prepared to return home.

"Now that we know one another," said Tournier, through interpreters, of course, "may we visit you someday in your home and talk of trade between our two peoples?"

Trotting Wolf thought deeply for a moment before answering.

"A decision has been made by my people," he said. "No one man has the authority to change that decision. When I return home, I'll tell everyone what happened here. We'll see. In the meantime, perhaps our traders will visit you here in the Valley Town of the Catawbas."

"Tout juste," said Tournier, and he gave a bow of his head.

Trotting Wolf turned to 'Squani.

"And what will you do now?" he asked.

'Squani looked at Osa.

"My home is gone," she said. "Let's go to yours."

"Uncle," said 'Squani to Trotting Wolf, swelling with pride, "my wife and I are coming home with you."

GLOSSARY

Cherokee words and phrases used in *The Dark Island*

Amayelequa, the big island, from *ama,* water + *ye,* a locative + *equa,* big. The "l" is inserted to prevent an unpleasant hiatus.

Ani-Asquani, Spanish people, or Spaniards, from *ani,* a plural prefix + *Asquani,* apparently a Cherokee attempt to render the Spanish *Español.*

Ani-Cusa, Creek or Muskogee People.

Ani-Kutani, the ancient priesthood of the Cherokees, killed off in a revolt of the people. The word *Kutani* cannot be translated.

Ani-Sawahani, Shawnees, or Shawnee People.

Ani-Tagwa, Catawba people.

Ani-Tsiksa, Chickasaw people.

Ani-Wahya, Wolf People, the Wolf Clan of the Cherokees.

Ani-yunwi-ya, the Real People, Cherokee designation for themselves *(ani,* plural prefix + *yunwi,* person + *ya,* real or original).

Asquani, a Spaniard, here also a man's name. See *Ani-Asquani.*

Catawba, not a Cherokee word. A southeastern Indian tribe.

Chalakee, the origin of this word is controversial, but it appears to be of Choctaw origin. A designation for the Real People, which likely found its way into the trade jargon of the old southeast and later evolved into the

English "Cherokee."

Chalaque, French or Spanish rendering of the word "Chalakee."

Cusabo, not a Cherokee word. A southeastern Indian tribe.

Howa, okay.

Kanati, also known as "the Great Hunter" or "First Man." Figure from Cherokee mythology. He is also associated with Thunder. His wife is Selu (see below).

Kanohenuh, a hominy drink made from corn, traditionally served to guests.

Kituwah, an ancient Cherokee town. The word cannot be translated. Thought to be the original Cherokee town, or "Mother Town." Cherokees also refer to themselves as *Ani-Kituwahgi* (Kituwah People). A traditional Cherokee society also goes by the name. The word is variously spelled, more often, contemporarily, Keetoowah.

Kutani, one of the ancient priests. See *Ani-Kutani.*

Osa, a Spanish word, "she-bear," the name of a character here.

Osiyo, a greeting. Can be translated "hello."

Sadayi, a woman's name.

Selu, corn, also the mythic "Corn Mother." See *Kanati.*

'Siyo, contracted form of *osiyo.*

'Squani, contracted form of *Asquani.*

Sawahani, a Shawnee.

Sogwili, a horse.

Timucua, not a Cherokee word. A Florida Indian tribe.

Uk'ten', contracted form of *ukitena,* a mythic Cherokee monster.

Usti, little, or a baby, i.e., little one.
Waccamaw, not a Cherokee word. A southeastern Indian tribe.
Wado, thank you.
Yansa, buffalo. More properly, the American bison.

Center Point Publishing
600 Brooks Road ● PO Box 1
Thorndike ME 04986-0001 USA

(207) 568-3717

US & Canada:
1 800 929-9108